In
Kate was the most ~~precious~~
figure in the church

The guests gasped and, at the altar, Kate froze. Then someone grabbed her from behind and dragged her toward the open door. She knew those strong arms, that spicy cedar smell. Mitch Connery had rescued her. Again.

Outside, sunshine turned his amber eyes to molten gold as he set her down and moved away. She felt a tug—not a delicate inner tug, but a sharp yank near her waistline.

They both glanced down and saw that somehow, during their close encounter, his belt buckle had tangled itself in the lace of her gown.

His hips swiveled tantalizingly close to her, and Kate could feel his heat reflecting...in places she'd never dared to associate with a man.

Dear Reader,

In the tiny Western town of Grazer's Corners, something is happening.... Weddings are in the air— and the town's most eligible bachelors are running for cover!

Three popular American Romance authors have put together a rollicking good time in THE BRIDES OF GRAZER'S CORNERS. This month it's Jacqueline Diamond's *The Cowboy & the Shotgun Bride*, then Mindy Neff with *A Bachelor for the Bride* and then Charlotte Maclay with *The Hog-Tied Groom*.

You're invited to all three weddings.... Who'll catch the bouquet next?

Happy reading!

Debra Matteucci
Senior Editor & Editorial Coordinator
Harlequin Books
300 East 42nd Street
New York, NY 10017

The Cowboy &
The Shotgun Bride

JACQUELINE DIAMOND

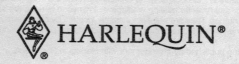

HARLEQUIN®

TORONTO • NEW YORK • LONDON
AMSTERDAM • PARIS • SYDNEY • HAMBURG
STOCKHOLM • ATHENS • TOKYO • MILAN • MADRID
PRAGUE • WARSAW • BUDAPEST • AUCKLAND

ISBN 0-373-16734-2

THE COWBOY & THE SHOTGUN BRIDE

Copyright © 1998 by Jackie Hyman.

All rights reserved. Except for use in any review, the reproduction or
utilization of this work in whole or in part in any form by any electronic,
mechanical or other means, now known or hereafter invented, including
xerography, photocopying and recording, or in any information storage
or retrieval system, is forbidden without the written permission of the
publisher, Harlequin Enterprises Limited, 225 Duncan Mill Road,
Don Mills, Ontario, Canada M3B 3K9.

All characters in this book have no existence outside the imagination of
the author and have no relation whatsoever to anyone bearing the same
name or names. They are not even distantly inspired by any individual
known or unknown to the author, and all incidents are pure invention.

This edition published by arrangement with Harlequin Books S.A.

® and TM are trademarks of the publisher. Trademarks indicated with
® are registered in the United States Patent and Trademark Office, the
Canadian Trade Marks Office and in other countries.

Printed in U.S.A.

Chapter One

"Aren't you glad nothing ever happens in Grazer's Corners?" asked the mayor, Moose Harmon, as he stood beaming at the town's only signal light. "You don't even have to risk getting shot."

The light, set into one corner of the town square, was positioned so as to halt traffic directly in front of Moose's department store. Lengthy delays in all directions gave motorists plenty of time to examine his display windows.

However, although Moose was gazing fondly at the signal, his words were not addressed to it. Kate Bingham wished that they were, so she could have him declared insane, break off their engagement, and get herself unelected sheriff.

"I know nothing about law enforcement," she growled through gritted teeth. "I'm an elementary school principal, in case you hadn't noticed."

"Oh, come on, Kate." Her fiancé favored her with a forlorn, puppylike gaze, which looked ridiculous on a hulking ex-linebacker. "After all the trouble I went to organizing a write-in vote, you've got to go along with this. Everybody knows old Sneed can't investigate his way out of a paper bag."

Kate opened her mouth to reply, then snapped it shut. She was familiar with Moose's plan, because he'd been yammering about it for months. He wanted to elect a figurehead, then hire a professional deputy to enforce the law in this small central California town.

Grazer's Corners was growing, with its agriculture-related businesses now augmented by a candy company, a toy manufacturer and a microprocessing firm. The old mom-and-pop grocery store had been replaced by two rival supermarkets, and yuppy housing developments were springing up on the outskirts. Could crime be far behind?

But why did Moose have to pick on her? And why had he chosen the June election, less than a week before their wedding?

Because, Kate told herself grimly, *he couldn't find anyone else to run. Besides, you can't bear to let people down, and he knows it.*

"You must have heard about the write-in campaign," Moose wheedled. "You never objected."

If the man hadn't towered more than a foot above her, Kate might have been tempted to give him a poke in the eye. She doubted a kick in the kneecap would vent her frustration sufficiently.

Instead, she pulled herself up to her full five feet two inches and glared at him. "I heard a rumor but I figured it was a joke. I had end-of-the-year awards to hand out, the fourth grade Sacramento trip to supervise, and a few other details occupying my mind. Like our wedding!"

"But now you'll have all summer to hire a deputy," Moose murmured. "After the honeymoon, of course."

Kate was almost tempted to tell him there wasn't

going to be a honeymoon. Moose had a kind and lovably daffy side, but sometimes he was downright infuriating.

Before she could frame a reply, he spoke again. "I've told you all the trouble we've been having with shoplifters. Do you want my store—our store—to go broke?"

It was true that Harmon's Department Store had suffered significant losses the previous quarter, mostly from out-of-towners passing through. Sheriff Sneed Brockner hadn't done anything beyond taking a report.

He preferred spending every spare minute in his heirloom garden, coaxing cabbage roses into bloom. It was Sneed himself, ten minutes ago, who had sarcastically congratulated Kate on her victory in yesterday's election and said he planned to celebrate by taking a tour of the state's botanical gardens. Starting immediately.

Then he'd slammed the door on his motor home and headed out of town. How childish, Kate thought, and how irresponsible.

He knew perfectly well that her term of office hadn't started yet. Besides, she didn't have a clue how to run a sheriff's department.

Moose was right about one thing: Grazer's Corners needed to hire a professional lawman. But he'd had no right to run her for office without permission.

She ought to tell him off and tender her resignation. But Kate knew she wouldn't.

Without hesitation, she would fight for a student with disabilities or go to bat for a teacher who needed compassionate leave. But when it came to herself, Kate Bingham was a thirty-one-year-old, power-suited, master's-degree-holding pushover.

"Besides," Moose teased, "didn't you always want to rule the world? Here's your big chance."

In spite of herself, Kate started to laugh. Okay, she *was* ambitious, for her students, anyway. She had almost single-handedly persuaded the board of education to let her upgrade the curriculum. She'd won the trust of the teaching staff, shanghaied parents into volunteering and already seen test scores begin to rise.

If she could handle the school board, she could certainly handle this nonsense about being elected sheriff. Kate brushed back a strand of straight, chin-length blond hair, and squared her shoulders.

"I suppose we could advertise for a deputy," she conceded. "If you cheapskates on the town council will spring for a decent salary."

"I was thinking of maybe a percentage," said Moose.

"A percentage of what?"

"What he saves us," said the mayor. "You know, in shoplifting losses and so forth."

Kate stared at Moose to see if he was joking. The man's tendency to be a skinflint was one of his less appealing qualities, but this was going a bit far. Maybe not all that far, though, for him.

Two years ago, right after he was elected mayor, Moose's store had stopped underwriting the cost of a professional band to play summer concerts in the park. The "local talent" who took its place had created a run on earplugs at the drugstore, but Moose still contended they added a down-home flavor.

Still, expecting law enforcement to work on commission was ridiculous. "Any deputy who would come here on that basis would have to be either crazy, incompetent or crooked," she said.

Moose sighed. "Well, maybe we can come up with a salary."

Down the block, Razz Fiddle placed a placard with today's specials in the window of the Good Eats Diner. The greasy spoon was unpopular among the owners of neighboring, more upscale shops, but when the graying ex-hippie waved at the mayor, Moose had no choice but to reply with his best running-for-reelection-in-November smile.

"Don't forget the benefits," said Kate.

The smile faded into a long-suffering look. She wondered whether it would wear better in ten or twenty years, and doubted it.

But he was hardworking and, like Kate, committed to their hometown. Grazer's Corners would be a perfect place to raise children, and she hadn't run across any better candidates for Daddy than her old high school boyfriend, Bledsoe Harmon, nicknamed Moose since his football days.

She lost her train of thought as a rusty brown van bearing Texas plates zipped along Raisin Road, next to the department store. It ran a red light and swerved directly in front of them.

A pickup truck carrying a small camper veered to avoid a collision and squealed to a halt with one tire on the sidewalk. The van stopped, but not before kicking up a breeze that etched a dust mote into one of Kate's contact lenses and sent her eye into an itchy fit.

"Well, sheriff?" boomed Moose. "Aren't you going to give them a ticket?"

Kate started to point out that her term of office wouldn't start until...well, she wasn't sure exactly.

But Sneed's hasty departure had left her as the only law in town, and she took her duties seriously.

"I haven't got a ticket book. I don't even know what one looks like. Still, that van could have hurt somebody." She rubbed her smarting eye, but that just made it water more. "I'll give them Lecture Number Five, the one about the same rules applying to everyone. If you insist."

"Uh..." Moose seemed to have gotten something stuck in his throat, but she doubted a mere dust mote would have done the trick. "Uh, maybe you better forget it, Kate." He backed away.

"Make up your mind, will you?" She turned toward the van, but a film of moisture obscured her vision.

"Kate, for heaven's sake..."

"I can handle this, Moose! You got me elected, so let me do my job!"

In front of her, three men formed blurs in the middle of the street. She couldn't tell much about them; in fact, their faces appeared almost featureless except for the eyes.

"Oh, for crying out loud!" Kate called to them. "You can't leave your van there. You're blocking the road!"

She heard Moose thump across the sidewalk behind her, scampering toward his store as if it had just caught fire and the year's profits were still inside. What was wrong with that man?

Trying to maintain her dignity despite the rapid blinking of her eyelids, Kate started toward the out-of-towners. "All right, which of you is the driver? I'll need to see your license and proof of insurance."

"Mah license?" came a voice with a twangy accent and a note of sheer disbelief.

Something else occurred to her. The men had piled out awfully fast. ''I don't think you were wearing your seat belts, either. We're very strict about that in California.''

All three men shifted slightly to the left and raised their right arms. They couldn't be holding up their hands to go to the bathroom, but what *were* they doing?

Someone rushed at Kate from the direction of the pickup truck, off to her left. Someone large and muscular, who caught her around the waist and yanked her out of the street just as a series of firecrackers went off.

At least, they sounded like firecrackers, but the Fourth of July was still a month away. Besides, Kate could have sworn she heard one of them whistle past her ear.

Across the square, a woman screamed. Up the block, a shop door slammed, and she could hear one of the Grand brothers who ran Grandma's Bakery yelling for people to get down.

The dust mote chose that moment, finally, to relinquish its perch on Kate's contact lens. She got one clear, heart-stopping glimpse of three men with bandannas over their faces and shotguns in their hands before she was jerked behind the truck.

''Oh, my gosh,'' she gasped. ''They were shooting at me!''

''I was beginning to wonder if you had a death wish, ma'am,'' drawled a masculine voice. It was deep and melodic and definitely did not belong to Moose.

''Oh, my gosh,'' Kate repeated, and felt herself starting to shake. This wouldn't do, she told herself sternly. ''Who are those guys?'' She remembered she'd never seen her rescuer before, either. "And who the heck are you?"

"Doesn't matter. If you'll just keep your head down, ma'am, I'll have them out of the way in no time."

Although the stranger probably stood no more than six feet tall, there was a calm intensity about his manner that made him seem larger than life. Perhaps that was due to his broad shoulders and muscular, home-on-the-range build, but Kate suspected it owed more to his personality.

"Do you have a cell phone?" she asked. "We need to call the—" The who?

"Sorry, I'm fresh out of phones." The man had the shaggy brown hair and deep tan of a cowboy. He wore a Stetson, a yoked shirt and leather vest, and, on the belt through his jeans, an ornate silver buckle. "But I've got something better."

"Better?" Hearing no more gunfire, Kate peered around the hood. To her dismay, the three men had fanned out and were closing in on the truck.

One was a big fellow who hulked forward. The second bandit, a thin grizzled man, limped as he walked. The third and youngest of the trio loped toward them with Ichabod Crane gawkiness and a triumphant leer on his bony face.

She couldn't believe they actually meant to shoot her, or anyone. Things like this didn't happen in Grazer's Corners.

Then, from inside the vest, her companion produced a sleek gun that looked high-tech, maybe even rapid-fire. It couldn't possibly be legal.

"Do you have a permit for that weapon?" she demanded.

"Do you care?"

Come to think of, she didn't.

He waited another moment, then bolted from the shelter of the truck and fired a rapid sequence of shots. Cursing, the three men scattered, and by the time they got their shotguns aimed, her rescuer had disappeared around the corner.

After a moment's consultation, two of the bandits ran after him. The third leaped into the van, wrenched it into gear and whipped around the corner in their wake.

Why hadn't the cowboy stayed here and shot them from the cover of the truck? Kate wondered. It would have been easier and safer.

But if he had, the men would have fired back in her direction. It was hard to imagine that this total stranger had intentionally drawn their fire away from Kate when her own fiancé had thought only of saving his own hide, but she supposed it was possible.

On the other hand, she'd gotten the impression that her rescuer didn't especially want to kill the bandits. With such a clear shot, he should have hit at least one of them. What was going on here?

From the building behind her, Moose called, "Kate! Come in, quick!" By sheer force of will, she managed to stand up, but her legs shook so badly she immediately grabbed the truck for support.

She felt like an idiot. Kate Bingham never displayed weakness. She was supposed to be a tower of strength, unfazed by education faddists and upchucking first graders alike.

What would the townspeople think? But then, the central park had fallen eerily quiet for a weekday morning. She doubted anyone other than Moose could see her, and he was in no position to criticize.

Kate was still hanging on to the reinforced bar of the side-view mirror when she heard the click of cowboy boots. Before she could turn, a hand clapped over her mouth, silencing her instinctive gasp of alarm.

It was a large hand, firm but gentle. It smelled faintly of cologne and cedar.

The man moved alongside her, and his concerned, amber-colored gaze met hers. The hand transferred itself to her elbow, steadying her tremors. "Didn't want you to scream, ma'am," said the cowboy. "Those varmints may be too stupid to keep an eye on my truck, but they aren't deaf."

Hearing his mellifluous baritone and feeling his touch blaze along her arm made Kate's knees quiver even harder. She wanted to retort that she never screamed, but then, her legs had never refused to obey her commands before, either.

"I'm—fine." To her chagrin, her voice came out quavery, like that of a little kid sent to the principal's office for throwing paper airplanes in class. "Shouldn't you—I mean, won't those guys…" She had to clamp her teeth together to keep them from chattering.

The man leaned against the truck as if trying to decide what to do with her. "You might be going into shock, ma'am. Is there a hospital in town?"

Of course there was, a few miles south on Almond Grove Avenue, but she didn't intend to tell him that. Kate Bingham being treated for shock? Never!

"I'm just—a little shaken." She took a couple of deep breaths. "Are those guys—after you? We should notify…" That was all she could squeeze out.

The creak of hinges told her Moose was prying open the department store's double doors at last. He must have decided it was safe to come out, or else he was afraid of what people would think.

"Do me a favor, ma'am." The amber eyes bored into hers. "If it's up to you, don't call the police just yet, will you? Give me half an hour, that's all I ask."

The request made no sense. Why didn't he want protection? "Whatever you say. But…"

"Is she all right?" Moose edged toward them.

"Is this lady related to you, sir?" inquired the stranger.

"She's my fiancée." The mayor's customary bluster crept back. "And I'll thank you to take your hand off her."

"That hand is supporting my elbow!" Kate snapped.

"I can see I'm interfering here." She could have sworn she glimpsed disappointment on the cowboy's face as he handed her to Moose, then rounded the truck. "You'd best get indoors before they return."

Kate didn't want to leave the scene just yet. Even if she hadn't been elected sheriff, she would still have felt an obligation to help this man who was obviously in trouble. But Moose pulled her toward the store, and at the moment she lacked the fortitude to stand on her own.

The truck roared to life. It made a quick circuit of the square and turned at the Corner Church, going west on Grape Street.

The most exciting man Kate had ever met was disappearing from her life. The warmth of his hand lingered on her arm, and she registered the memory of his soft breath whispering across her cheek.

Who was he? And why did she have the sense that a great adventure had just passed her by?

Moose tugged her the rest of the way into the store. They had barely cleared the threshold when the van roared up.

It paused for a second as if the occupants were staring at the space where the truck used to be. Then, through its open windows, a stream of cuss words befouled the air.

"Cover your ears!" Moose yanked the door shut. "You didn't catch that, did you, Kate?"

She couldn't believe he was more concerned about her hearing a few barnyard phrases than he had been about the possibility of her getting shot. As the van sped down Almond Grove Avenue, Kate's voice, and her temper, returned full force.

"Why, you big oaf!" she sputtered as the store employees poked their heads from behind the counters. "You left me out there to get killed!"

"You told me to," Moose protested.

"I did not!"

"You told me to go away and let you do your job." He sounded hurt. "I was trying to respect you as a professional."

"A professional what?" she growled. "I couldn't see a darn thing, the way my contact was hurting. You left me out there helpless!"

"I didn't know you couldn't see!"

"You knew I was facing three masked gunmen!"

"I'm really sorry, Kate." Moose hung his head sheepishly. "At first I figured it might be some kind of trick you were playing, to pay me back for the election. Then I kind of panicked."

It was a plausible explanation. In the face of his

contrition, Kate could feel her fury waning, but she didn't intend to let him off the hook that easily. "A total stranger showed more concern for my safety than my own fiancé! I don't see how I can ever trust you again!"

Behind the makeup counter, Betsy Muller crouched, her heavily lined eyes widening hopefully. There was one strand of purple in her dyed-platinum hair, and this was the one she twisted around her finger as she waited breathlessly.

The young woman had nursed an unrequited crush on Moose for years. She'd gone into a deep funk as the wedding date approached, and now the possibility of a broken engagement must loom like a last-minute reprieve.

But did Kate really want to end her relationship with Moose? The cowboy was long gone. Even if he turned up again, he hardly struck her as marriage material for an elementary school principal.

"Well..." She tapped her foot as she tried to frame an appropriate reproach.

"I made a mistake." The admission startled her, coming from a man who was usually expert at stone-walling. "I didn't think, Kate. Please forgive me."

"I guess it was kind of hard to sort out what was happening," she heard herself say.

"As for that cowboy, I'd say he bears checking out," Moose continued, picking up steam now that forgiveness was in sight.

"He's not the one who tried to shoot me!" Kate said.

"We should report those bandits, too," Moose added quickly. "They're probably all heading down

Route 59 toward the freeway. I'll call the highway patrol.''

Kate remembered her rescuer's request to delay calling anyone for half an hour. Unless she found good reason to do otherwise, she intended to honor it.

"I'll call them myself," she said. As Moose reached into his pocket for his cell phone, she added, "From the sheriff's department. Excuse me. I've got a job to do."

Head high, she strode out of the store. On the sidewalk, a moment's queasiness struck as she noted a bullet hole in the window at the *Grazer Gazette,* the town's weekly paper. It reminded her of how close she'd come to being mowed down.

She gave a prayer of thanks that neither she nor anyone else had been injured. Already, people were emerging from the bank and the bakery, searching for damage and, judging by the expansive hand gestures, embroidering their own narrow escapes.

In a sense, those intruders had done the town a favor, she mused with a glint of humor. As Moose had said earlier, Grazer's Corners was a quiet place. This would give people something to talk about for at least a week.

Kate walked around the square toward town hall, which stood opposite the department store. In the park, a sudden gust of wind set the flag to flapping sharply, and she jumped.

She had to get her nerves under control. People depended on Kate to stay calm, and she couldn't let them down.

To her relief, no one came out of the newspaper office as she passed. The sidewalk in front of town hall was deserted as well, and Kate slipped unnoticed into the courtyard of the Spanish-style complex. Already, she felt a little steadier.

A fountain bubbled halfheartedly in the sunshine, and a couple of pigeons pecked at the courtyard's tile floor. The door to the town clerk's office stood open, and Kate could hear someone talking inside.

As she came closer along the walkway, she recognized the dry, cracked voice of the clerk, Agatha Flintstone, a seventyish lady who also owned the town's bookstore. Kate glanced inside, right through the empty outer office and into Agatha's chamber, where the clerk sat in profile at her desk, so absorbed in a book she didn't seem to realize she was reading aloud.

"Gleaming in his armor, the knight loomed above her, his lance erect..." The town clerk fluffed her gray hair, which was already teased to near Marge Simpson heights. "Her bosom heaved as she contemplated his massive presence..." Absently, she tugged at the neckline of her homemade, flowered smock.

Kate hurried past, loath to be caught snooping even though Agatha made no secret of her fantasies about being ravished by a Norman conqueror. It was said that Sneed Brockner's ego had shriveled years ago as a result of being inspected daily and found wanting.

Fantasy could be healthy, as Kate reminded parents when they criticized the recommended reading lists. Not every book had to be reality-based. Given Agatha's minutely ordered life, no wonder she sought escape in make-believe.

And my life? she wondered as she neared the sheriff's department. *Isn't it just as stifling?*

A vision seized her, of Moose's two-story stucco house in the northern part of town. In her mind, barbed wire topped the ironwork perimeter fence and bars covered the windows. Peering out, as from a prison, was Kate's own bleak face.

What on earth was wrong with her? How could a chance encounter with a cowboy make her yearn for—for something she couldn't name? Adventure, maybe. The unexpected. Tingles that crept along her nerve endings, and heat that flooded her body.

Kate could still smell his cologne and see the concern in his gaze. His frame wasn't massive, like Moose's, but tightly packed and protective. If only she could feel those strong arms around her one more time, and listen to that deep fluid voice!

Whoever those bandits had been, surely they would get caught sooner or later. Once he was rid of them, perhaps the stranger would remember a woman he'd saved in Grazer's Corners, a small, slender lady with swingy hair and dreamy eyes—at least, she hoped they'd looked dreamy rather than red-rimmed and irritated—and he would come back and run his hands along her shoulders until she melted against him.

Good lord, she was worse than Agatha! Dismayed, Kate lifted her chin and opened the door.

"Hi! I was hoping you'd drop by." Jeanie Jeffrey, the clerk-dispatcher, beamed at Kate from behind the stacks of flyers, reports and mail littering her desk.

The battered office smelled musty, probably because the only window had been painted shut long ago. Jeanie, who happily described herself as a burrowing creature, disliked both fresh air and sunshine. Also filing, Kate noted.

On a bulletin board, several ragged Wanted posters were half-covered by announcements of country club dances and school carnivals, now long past. A ring of keys, one of which no doubt opened the town's only jail cell, hung conspicuously on a nail.

Kate bit back the instinct to tear into this mess. She wasn't even officially the sheriff yet.

"You didn't call for backup, did you?" she asked.

"Backup?" asked Jeanie blankly. "For a bunch of firecrackers going off?"

"It was a shoot-out," Kate said. "But no one got hurt."

"No kidding!" Jeanie's face lit up. "Wow! Think it'll be on TV tonight?"

"Not unless we're fielding invisible camera crews from Modesto these days," Kate replied. "I don't suppose you've received any All Points Bulletins from Texas lately, have you?"

"APBs. Hmm." Jeanie regarded the sheets of paper littering the floor beneath the fax machine. "Could be one in there. Let me check."

"Never mind." Hurrying around the desk, Kate scooped them up. For some reason, she felt reluctant to have anyone else see them.

She flipped through the bulletins. There was one from Orange County, another from San Diego. Portland, Oregon. Las Vegas.

Even before she noticed that the issuing agency was the Gulch City, Texas, police department, the photograph stopped her. The hair hadn't yet grown shaggy and the eyes lacked the wariness she'd seen, but it was unmistakably him.

Her stranger. Her rescuer. The man she had imagined might come riding back to sweep Kate Bingham into his arms.

His name was Mitch Connery. And he was wanted for murder.

Chapter Two

The date of the murder was one week earlier. A man had been shot to death, perhaps with the same gun Mitch Connery had used today.

Kate's mouth went dry as she read the particulars. The victim was one Jules Kominsky, age 38, occupation cowboy.

Could he have been a friend of the three bandits? That might explain their murderous rage toward Mitch.

She skimmed the description of the crime, instinctively translating the law-enforcement terminology into standard English. According to the Gulch City police, Mitch Connery had been involved in a legal dispute regarding a ranch he had formerly owned. One week ago, he had attempted to break into the ranch house and was confronted by the victim, whom he shot.

It sounded so cut-and-dried. But how could the police be sure what had happened that night on the ranch? What if Kominsky had fired first?

On the other hand, that didn't excuse Mitch's breaking into the place. And, if he was innocent, surely he wouldn't have fled.

She realized she must have skipped over his occupation, and reread the bulletin. Now, there was a surprise! Mitch was listed as an attorney.

She could hardly believe the man who'd come galloping, or rather driving, into her life today was a paper-shuffler. He'd been—she checked the bulletin to confirm her impression—six feet of sheer muscle, with the tanned leanness you'd expect from a man who'd spent thirty-five years living outdoors.

According to the bulletin, the fugitive was considered armed and dangerous. Yet he'd risked his life to pull her to safety.

Dangerous? she wondered with a shiver. Only to her peace of mind.

Still, she had an obligation as a citizen, even if she wasn't yet a sworn officer of the law, to report what had happened. Since half an hour had passed, she wouldn't be betraying her promise.

Kate put in a phone call to the California Highway Patrol. A dispatcher took down the information on the shoot-out and promised to alert officers to look for the van.

Despite a tremor of guilt, Kate omitted any mention of Mitch's name or the fact that he was wanted for murder. She didn't call Gulch City, either.

If people believed he was armed and dangerous, they might shoot first and ask questions later. He had saved her life. She owed him that much.

She debated whether to fill out a report, since she wasn't yet officially sheriff. It seemed irresponsible not to, however, so she obtained a form from Jeanie and wrote down as much as she could remember. She didn't feel up to interviewing witnesses, though, not while she was still having trouble keeping her hand steady.

Kate gave the report to the dispatcher with a sense of relief. It would probably end up at the bottom of a stack of papers, but at least she had done her duty.

Mitch Connery and the Gang That Couldn't Shoot Straight had hightailed it out of Grazer's Corners. Kate would never see them again.

The thought gave her a hollow sensation, probably another aftereffect of shock. True, she wished she knew more about Mitch's past, and what had really happened that night at the ranch house.

But it was simple curiosity, nothing more.

SOMETHING WAS WRONG with the way she looked.

Kate stared into the mirror in the church's small conference room, which she was using as a dressing room. A heavier-than-usual dose of eye makeup had set her contacts on edge, and she kept blinking as she tried to figure out what was amiss.

Her hair seemed limper than usual beneath its circlet of roses, but that wasn't it. The dress that had struck her as elegantly simple now appeared too fussy with its high-necked silk bodice, transparent sleeves and the skirt layered with white-on-white embroidery and lace. But that wasn't the problem either, not exactly.

Her glance fell on the bouquet. Jammed together, the roses and baby's breath had lost any fresh garden beauty they might ever have possessed. They looked like captives. Claustrophobic. Squashed.

Kate's mind flashed on the image she'd formed a few days earlier, of Moose's house with the windows barred. What was wrong, she realized with a start, wasn't her appearance, it was her sense that she was walking into a prison.

She wished her parents were here to advise her. Linda Bingham had been a teacher, Kate's inspiration. She'd married her childhood sweetheart, a businessman, and he had shared his wife's deep-rooted values.

Her parents had died within a year of each other, but they'd left behind their deep love for their daughter and for their community.

And, Kate reminded herself, Moose shared her affection for Grazer's Corners. He understood how important the school and her students were to her, too. Why, he was the only guy she'd ever met whom she would even consider as a husband.

Except for a man with tender brown eyes and a hard, lean body. If I were a passionate sort of woman, he could set me on fire with one glance.

Where had that thought come from? Kate smiled nervously at herself in the mirror. Some people might say she was frustrated from saving herself for her wedding night, although it had never seemed like a burden before this.

After tonight, she would never fantasize about strangers again, she reminded herself. She would have Moose all to herself, and somehow the miracle of marriage would transform him into all the things a man should be, sexy and exciting and tender, just like…just like…

A light knock startled her. "Yes?"

"Dressed?" The door cracked open and the bright face of Charity Arden peered inside. A camera dangled from a strap around her neck. "I'd like to take a couple of 'before' shots."

"Sure." Kate started to wipe her hands on her skirt and then thought the better of it. "Is the church full?"

"Everybody's here, just about." Charity, who free-lanced at weddings when she wasn't shooting for the *Grazer Gazette,* sauntered into the room. She was tall and pretty, with golden brown hair and a heart-shaped face, although she never seemed to take much interest in her appearance. "They're still buzzing about the shoot-out."

There had been no news regarding the cowboy or his pursuers, and Kate preferred not to dwell on the incident. "I hear your editor is going to preserve the piece of glass with the bullet hole and hang it as a souvenir."

"Just rumors. At least, I hope so." With a grin, Charity went to work positioning her subject in the soft natural light streaming through a window.

Kate yearned for a reassuring circle of bridesmaids, but selecting them would have created an impression of favoritism. Most of her friends were teachers from her own classroom days, and some were among the instructional staff she now supervised.

Charity quickly put her at ease, however, snapping away and chatting at the same time. As usual, the young photographer was casually dressed in a long denim skirt and a khaki fisherman's vest replete with pockets for film and filters. Her one concession to the dressy occasion was the lace-trimmed blouse underneath.

"You look just perfect, honey," the photographer observed as she framed a shot. "Radiant."

"Really?" Kate was surprised at how deceptive appearances could be.

"I just adore seeing people fall madly in love and plan their futures together." Charity sounded wistful.

Madly in love? That wasn't quite how Kate felt about Moose. Affectionate, yes. Aware of shared values and goals. Those were the things that counted in the long run, weren't they?

Rashness wasn't part of Kate's nature. She couldn't imagine herself throwing conventionality to the winds, the way Charity had done when she conceived her seven-year-old son and then insisted on keeping him.

The town gossips still liked to speculate, but no one had ever figured out his paternity, and Charity wasn't talking. Not about that, anyway.

Someone rapped on the door with military precision. "Is the bride ready?" boomed a male voice. "Let's get this show on the road!"

That would be Maynard Grazer, the president of the school board. A wealthy descendant of the town's founders, he owned stables and vineyards just outside town and was considered something of a local patriarch. He had also backed Kate when she applied to be elementary school principal.

Unsure who should walk her down the aisle, she had decided it would be a nice gesture to ask Maynard. He had replied that he could use the practice, since his own daughter, Jordan, would be getting married the following Saturday. It was as close as Maynard ever came to making a joke.

"I'm ready, I guess." As she opened the door, Kate hoped neither Charity nor Maynard noticed the equivocation in her response.

She let the photographer exit first, then stepped into the vestibule. Maynard made a reassuringly solid figure in his tuxedo, his once-youthful good looks now tempered by extra weight and graying hair but his bearing still straight and proud. When he offered his arm, Kate placed her gloved hand atop it gratefully.

The foyer of the Spanish-style church stood empty. From the sanctuary, Kate could hear "We've Only Just Begun," harmoniously rendered by the town's choirmaster, who doubled as organist.

Charity must have signaled him, because the melody switched to "Here Comes the Bride." And here, with a deep breath, she came.

Dead ahead, before the altar, waited Moose, his face flushed and his shoulders thrown back. The cockeyed position of his bow tie gave the tuxedo a comical air, which somehow made her feel better.

Behind him, the aged pastor, the Reverend Louis Lewis, beamed vaguely and with great dignity at his congregation. Perpetually on the brink of turning eighty, the Rev. Lewis seemed to have been pickled in the jar of time. Gossip suggested that he had been exactly the same age and held the same position since the town's founding in 1910.

Kate spared a glance for Jordan Grazer, sitting beside her future husband, banker Randall Latrobe. They made a handsome pair, Jordan dark and sweet-faced, Randall blond and sleek.

Jordan's eyes met Kate's for a flick of a second. Was that unhappiness in them? Could Jordan be entertaining the same sort of doubts as Kate?

Just beyond her sat the other couple who would be married this month, in two weeks' time. Garrett Keeley, who had the rugged appeal of a former star quarterback, radiated self-assurance. It was hard to read much in the reserved, model-perfect face of his fiancée, socialite Hailey Olson.

But then, Kate told herself, none of the Grazer's Corners brides and grooms were so immature as to expect to live out a fairy tale. They were marrying someone respectable and would take their proper places in the life of the town.

Just like her. And that was as it should be. She was older than this month's other two brides, ready to settle down, and doing the right thing by marrying Moose.

Then Kate glimpsed a man sitting to one side, near the front. The man who had haunted her dreams for the past three nights, whose searing touch remained imprinted on her arm. The man who should never have come back.

He sat twisted in his pew, his steely gaze sweeping the church. His eyes touched on her face in surprise, and Kate nearly missed her step, but Maynard steadied her and they surged forward.

Mitch Connery, wanted criminal, had crashed her wedding. But why? Who or what did he expect to find here?

There was nothing in the etiquette books, she felt certain, about how to deal with such a situation. However, Kate had read somewhere that when the unthinkable happened, it was best to ignore it. Besides, in her current state of mind, she could come up with no better course of action.

She and Maynard reached the altar. Moose blinked, gulped and helped her up the steps. Instinctively, Kate reached to straighten his bow tie, and heard a murmur of amusement run through the guests.

Oh, well. There was no sense in pretending she was too carried away to notice such a detail, when everyone here had known her and Moose since childhood.

Kate found herself glancing at the stranger. A faint frown etched across his forehead. When he realized she was looking, he cocked his head and raised one eyebrow as if to ask, Why?

Indignation roared through her. Did this cowboy, this fugitive, this...this...*lawyer* presume to question her judgment?

Kate put her hand in Moose's and faced the minister. The Reverend Louis Lewis pushed his wire-rimmed spectacles higher on his nose and fumbled with his Bible.

"Dearly beloved," said his scratchy voice. "We are gathered, uh..." A piece of paper slipped to the floor.

Moose bent over to scoop it up. Kate thought she heard, but hoped she was wrong, the sandpaper rasp of stitches parting. Behind her, people stirred, and a couple of coughs might have covered titters.

Then the world, if not Moose's pants, tore asunder.

The sanctuary's side door banged open, sunshine flooded the church and three ill-matched silhouettes stumped in. In the blazing glare, they might have been three demons risen from hell.

Kate recognized the shapes: the big, hulking one, the thin one with the limp and the lanky, long-necked one. She also recognized the outlines of shotguns clutched in their hands.

A sense of unreality held her, and everyone else, motionless. Then the reverend squinted toward the doorway and said, "Would the latecomers please take a seat so we may continue the service?"

"We're not leaving without him!" grunted one of the men, and swung his shotgun toward Mitch Connery.

But Mitch wasn't sitting in his pew anymore. He

must have dived for the floor and crawled for his life, judging by the way people were swiveling and side-stepping in the row ahead.

"Hand him over or y'all will pay!" whooped the gangly bandit, and fired into the ceiling.

The noise exploded through the room like a chain reaction. Women screamed. A couple of people in the back dashed out. A man cursed, but was quickly shushed.

In the front row, Maynard Grazer loomed to his feet. "Now see here!" he began, when his daughter let out a cry from where she sat with her fiancé.

"Daddy, don't!" wailed Jordan. "They'll kill you!"

The large bandit swung his gun toward the school board president. Kate's throat clenched in horror, and then she saw something small—about the size of a roll of film—fly through the air from one side and smack the gunman in the temple.

He stumbled, and his shot went wild. Charity Arden ducked behind a curtain, and Jordan Grazer rushed to her father's side. Maynard appeared stunned, but unharmed.

The church seethed as people ducked for cover. In the shuffling and shoving, it was no longer possible to trace Mitch's movements.

The bandits, whom she could now see were wearing bandannas, fanned out through the sanctuary, poking at people and peering under the pews. The young one kept shouting threats, but his Texas accent was so thick Kate couldn't understand half of what he said.

She felt an absurd impulse to call for order. Then it penetrated her dazed brain that she wasn't the principal, these weren't unruly students and she was standing here gaping like an idiot.

"Come on!" Moose called while piloting the baffled minister toward an inner door. "Get a move on!"

"Right." Kate took one step and nearly tripped over her many-layered skirt. Grimly, she collected it in one hand and began descending from the dais.

The harsh, angled light distorted her sense of depth, and she had to move cautiously. Then, across the room, another shot hit the ceiling, and the tumult abated.

"Everybody down!" yelled the tall, gangly bandit, who managed to torture at least three syllables from the word *down.*

Kate froze. She was stuck on the steps, the most prominent and exposed figure in the church. Should she sit? Finish making her way to the floor? Just stand here?

The older, grizzled gunman noticed her dilemma. Or rather, he saw his opportunity.

"Well, now," he drawled as he limped up the aisle toward her. "I don't suppose you want to see this sweet young bride harmed, now do you, Connery, you murdering varmint? So you just come out now, or I'll—"

From the direction of the curtains, a plastic film can flew with such deadly accuracy that the bandit might have had a bull's-eye painted on his forehead. In the split second in which the entire church was focused on his startled figure, someone grabbed Kate and dragged her toward the open door.

She knew those strong arms, and that spicy cedar smell. Mitch Connery had rescued her again.

The largest of the intruders thudded toward them

down the side aisle. Kate flung her bouquet wildly at him, but it flew instead into the arms of Jordan Grazer, who regarded it in confusion.

However, the hefty bandit had the misfortune to be passing Agatha Flintstone. Pulling a book from her purse, the town clerk whacked him in the side of the head so hard he staggered.

The elderly woman let out a whoop that reminded Kate of Mel Gibson in *Braveheart*. Around the church, people began howling and flinging things at the crooks.

"Let's get you out of here," growled Mitch.

They had reached the threshold when Charity Arden dashed forward, camera clicking as her news instincts came to the fore. Kate hoped the young woman got a good shot of her and Mitch; after her bold and life-saving accuracy, she deserved a reward.

Then they were outside in the blinding light, and Charity slammed the door behind them. It wouldn't slow the bandits for long, but every little bit helped.

Half a block away, Kate saw Charity's brother, Bud, struggling to parallel-park a panel truck bearing the logo of the family pig farm. She wasn't sure why he'd come late—Bud had been so moody these past few weeks that even his sister had remarked on it—but his present position blocked the bandits' van and would probably slow them even further.

"The best thing I can do for you, ma'am, is to make myself scarce," the cowboy said in a regretful baritone as he loosened his grip on Kate. "But my advice is to marry somebody else. Your fellow's chickened out on you twice."

"He saved the minister!" Kate retorted.

"It's your decision, ma'am. I don't mean to interfere.'' Sunshine turned Mitch Connery's amber eyes to molten gold as he released her. The June air felt cold as it rushed to take his place.

Kate felt a tug as he moved away. Not a delicate interior tug, but a sharp yank near her waistline. ''Hey!''

They both glanced down and saw the same thing. Somehow, during their close encounter, his belt buckle had worked its way into the lace of her skirt.

The man's hips swiveled tantalizingly close to hers. Kate could feel his heat reflecting in places she'd never dared to associate with a man, not until her wedding night.

She fumbled furiously with her gown. ''What a mess! You'll have to take it off!''

''Excuse me?'' He cocked his head.

''Your belt!''

''Oh. Yes, ma'am.'' Standing so close she could almost hear his blood thrumming, Mitch jerked on the buckle, but the prong was caught in the fabric. ''Sorry. It looks like I'll have to resort to brute force.''

''Don't you dare!'' But she could see they had no choice. What did a little bit of lace matter, anyway?

With a muttered apology, Mitch grabbed his belt in one hand and her skirt in another, and wrenched. If anything, the buckle twisted even deeper into the fabric.

Kate had years of experience in disentangling and unknotting and de-chewing-gumming all sorts of things, and she could see that this buckle and this skirt had well and truly mated. They would not be parted without scissors or a great deal of time, time that she and the cowboy didn't have.

Mitch must have drawn the same conclusion, because before she knew it they were both heading for his pickup, hopping along like two picnickers in a three-legged race. Like it or not, Kate would have to go with him until they could sort out their clothing.

Not only go with him, but sit practically in his lap. Worse, she discovered as they crammed into the front seat, she had to position herself sideways, her stomach pressed to his hip and her legs entwined with his.

At this close range, she got a front-row experience of how a man's body moves when he starts a truck. His muscles tighten, and he stretches out his thigh when he presses the accelerator, and as he shifts, his arm brushes the all-too-sensitive breast of any woman who happens to be pasted against him.

She also got a glancing view in the side mirror of the bandits bursting from the church, guns blazing. Down the street, Bud ducked out of sight, his vehicle still partly blocking the van.

Bullets blasted by, and Kate said a silent prayer of gratitude for the camper in the truck bed, which shielded Mitch's rear window. And for the fact that it didn't occur to those idiots to shoot out the pickup's tires.

The truck screeched around a corner, centrifugal force pressing Kate hard into Mitch. She'd never felt so aware of a man physically, even in years of stolen kisses and slow dancing with Moose.

"I figure by now somebody's got to have called the police, or the sheriff, whatever you folks do for law enforcement around here," Mitch said as he whipped onto first one side street and then another, zigzagging north of the square.

"Unfortunately," she said, "I'm the sheriff."

He hit the brakes, bringing the truck to a thumping

halt in the shade of a eucalyptus. "Ma'am," he said, "you have got to be kidding."

"I wish I were." On the verge of an explanation, Kate stopped herself. She saw no reason to reveal the full extent of Moose's shenanigans to this stranger. "In any case, we're not used to this sort of activity in Grazer's Corners."

"Ma'am, I realize that, but..." He stared through the windshield with a look so piercing it could probably be used for laser surgery. "I'm afraid there's something you need to know about me."

Sitting here, they were likely to be dead before he got through his confession, if that was what he intended to make. "Just turn right at the next corner and keep heading southeast," Kate said. He remained still. "We'll talk shortly," she assured him. "Now get moving, Mr. Mitch Connery of Gulch City, Texas."

The cowboy's jaw worked silently. Then he pressed the gas pedal and followed her directions.

By the time he spoke again, his lower eyelids had pouched up as if he were squinting over a prairie. "You taking me in, ma'am?"

"This isn't the way to the jail," she said. "I hardly ever lock up people who save my life. In fact, if they save it twice, I usually listen to their story before I decide what to do with them."

His taut mouth curved into an appreciative smile. "You do have a way with words, ma'am."

"My name is Kate," she said.

"Nice name."

"As opposed to what?"

"Tiffany. Bambi. Something typically California. Kate's a nice, serviceable name."

She blew a wisp of stray hair from her mouth.

"Mitch isn't bad, either. I guess you use Mitchell when you're arguing in front of the Supreme Court, though."

His laughter rumbled through her bones. "Mostly I draft people's wills and try to talk them out of divorces. Or weddings, in the present case."

Kate took a deep breath, then realized that, pressed so close, he could probably feel the rise and fall of her chest almost as well as she could. "Let's leave me out of this, all right?"

"If you say so, ma'am." The truck veered around the elementary school, slowing to twenty-five miles per hour even though it was summer and there were no children present.

The sight of her home-away-from-home steadied Kate. No matter how chaotic life became anywhere else, she always felt in charge there.

But she couldn't think about that today. She had to get herself disentangled, figure out what to do with Mitch and then...

Then what? Go back to the church and marry Moose?

She owed it to the man. He'd been loyal for years, waiting patiently and respecting Kate's decision to save herself. Maybe he wasn't some romantic hero, but he didn't deserve to be abandoned at the altar.

Of course, in a sense, he'd abandoned *her* at the altar. Had the reverend really needed help, or had he simply presented such an obstacle to Moose's escape route that it was easier to take him along than to go around?

She couldn't puzzle it out, could only stare through the window and try to decide what to do next. They were entering a familiar neighborhood of California bungalows built in the 1920s and '30s. The friendliness of the porches, many flanked by rosebushes in bloom, made her feel better.

"Mind telling me how much farther we're going?" Mitch asked.

With a start, Kate realized she was guiding him toward her own house. Well, why not? Under the circumstances, who would think to look for her at home?

"We're nearly there. Turn left at this street and then right into the second driveway. It curves around the back so no one can see the truck."

He did as she instructed, cornering past the mailbox designed as a red schoolhouse and bumping along her gravel drive. Behind the house, the engine died to silence in a small apple grove that her father had planted years ago.

Kate felt Mitch's heart rate decelerate as he took in the sheltering trees and rambling lot, the screened rear porch and the flower bed bursting with pansies. "This your home, Kate?"

She nodded. "I've got a key hidden. We can go inside and talk—once we get our clothes straightened out."

He made no move to separate them. "You planning to live here with that groom of yours?"

A wry chuckle escaped her. "Moose has a bigger place on the west side of town. He wouldn't live in a little cottage like this."

Mitch rested his head back against the seat. He made a slight gesture with his left hand as if to adjust a Stetson, but it wasn't there.

The cowboy hat, Kate realized, sat on the passenger seat to her right. Its well-worn softness and clean, brushed surface made it clear how high it placed in his affections.

Why on earth had this man given up being a cowboy for writing wills? Why had he turned to breaking into ranches and shooting people? "Did you do it?" she asked abruptly. "Kill that guy?"

Mitch's lips pressed together, hard. The planes of his face hardened, and suddenly he looked like a different man from the affable companion of the past few minutes. A cold man, and a desperate one.

What an idiot she'd been! She had brought a fugitive to this secluded place, where no one might come for days. She had no weapon; they might as well be handcuffed together for all the chance she had of escaping; and she'd just issued a direct challenge.

"Getting worried?" His tone sounded dangerously low.

Her throat went dry. "What makes you think that?"

"Ma'am, we're so close right now that a century ago we'd have been forced to get married to save your reputation," he murmured. "I can feel you getting all knotted up."

"Did you?" she repeated. "Kill him?"

To her amazement, Mitch began to laugh. "You are one cool customer, Madam Sheriff. No wonder these folks elected you. And yes, I did."

"Yes?" she repeated in disbelief.

"I shot Jules Kominsky," said the man whose leg was rubbing her hip and whose arm made an indentation just below her breast. "Shot him dead in the middle of the night, in somebody else's ranch house. Now, what are you going to do about it?"

Chapter Three

Mitch wondered for a minute if he had stated the case too baldly. But if he were going to trust this perplexing, fascinating lady with his whole story, he needed to know what kind of stuff she was made of.

Not that he didn't already have a clue. He'd never seen a woman with so much starch in her backbone.

At the same time, his instincts told him she could be so warm and compliant a man might lose himself in her. He had to suppress the urge to wriggle like an antsy schoolboy before she became aware of just how intensely his body was responding to their closeness.

"What am I going to do about it?" she repeated, her lips a few inches from his ear. "I'm going to let you tell me about the mitigating circumstances, and explain who these bandits were and why you crashed my wedding."

"That sounds fair." He almost managed to keep his breathing even.

"But first, do you have a pocket knife?" she said. "My leg is going to sleep and I've got a cramp in my back."

He didn't want to cut her loose. He wanted to demonstrate his Texas prowess, and watch those cool blue eyes of hers turn violet with hunger, and hear her no-nonsense voice hoarsen with cries of ecstasy.

This was no time to daydream, Mitch told himself. "A pocket knife? Yes, ma'am, if you'll just bear with me."

He reached for the glove compartment. This involved leaning across Kate, or rather, around and through her, since they were so inextricably entwined as to be virtually a new life form.

As he stretched, Mitch's cheek grazed her shoulder. The slight contact was enough to rev his rebellious body for action, the kind of action he didn't want to think about.

He must be crazy to have these kinds of feelings for another man's bride. Heck, she was also the person most likely to slap handcuffs on him and send him back to face a figurative lynching in Gulch City. That reflection dashed across him like a cold shower. He was just congratulating himself on cooling off, when, as he reached into the glove box, his forearm brushed a soft, tempting pair of breasts.

Blood rushed to his head and to other, less rational parts. "Excuse me," he muttered.

"Just get the darn thing," she growled, "and cut me loose."

"Yes, ma'am." Mitch lifted out the knife and sat up. He was about to pull the blade from the handle when Kate's hand closed over his wrist. "Better let me do that," she said.

Had he wanted to take command, there was no way she could have stopped him. Kate's hand was slim compared to his large, rough one, and her fingers didn't even close completely around his wrist.

All the more reason for him to be gentle, Mitch

thought. Besides, he preferred not to be the one who ruined her wedding dress.

"It's your call, sheriff," he said, and let her take the knife.

She flicked it open. "It looks sharp. You keep your equipment well-maintained."

"I used to be a cowboy. That's one of the things you learn first," Mitch said.

As she bent to saw her way free, he caught the light fragrance of roses from the band around Kate's hair. There was something innocent and free about the scent that reminded him of childhood and first love and a woman waiting to be awakened.

But not this one. Sheriff Kate was both engaged and old enough to know what she was doing. Heck, she and her fiancé had probably been doing it for years.

What could she see in that oaf who'd ducked off the altar so fast he nearly bowled over the minister? Well, that was her business, and Mitch intended to stay out of it.

Kate gave no sign of distress as she worked the blade through the strands of lace. The delicate bonds parted, leaving an unlovely hole in the beautiful dress and setting him free.

Mitch scooted back. He should have felt relief, but knew regret instead. He'd never get that close to her again, that was for sure.

Kate folded the blade and returned it to the dashboard. "I just learned a great deal about you, Mr. Connery."

"You better call me Mitch or I might think you're addressing the ghost of my father," he said. "What exactly have you learned?"

"You had the knife. You could have forced me out

of the truck and taken off," she said. "But you gave it to me, instead."

"Call me a sentimental fool." He tried to smile jauntily.

She slid away from him across the seat, sparing only a brief sorrowful glance at the wreckage of her skirt. "Coffee?"

"Sure. Let me help you down."

"Why? Should I worry about ripping my dress?" She transferred his Stetson to the dashboard, shoved the door wide and jumped down.

As he watched her approach the house, Mitch realized that Kate had just presented him with a golden opportunity. Now he could drive off without even having to threaten the sheriff.

She knew it, too. She stopped near the porch and regarded him for one cool moment. Then she crouched down and removed a loose brick from the foundation of the porch, and pulled out a key.

She was the darndest sheriff he'd ever met. Willing to trust a fugitive, and even let him into her house. That didn't mean she would let him get away without coming after him, though.

Mitch wiped his forehead on his sleeve and stared at the ignition. All he had to do was turn the key and be on his way.

But he hadn't found what he sought at the wedding. At this point, he'd be running blind.

The past week had gone by so fast, he'd barely had time to think. Heading west had been sheer instinct. That, and the only possible chance to clear himself.

So far, he had nothing but a few bullet holes in his camper to show for it. Billy Parkinson's gang might be blundering fools, but they'd nearly caught him twice now.

At first, he'd figured finding Loretta Blaine would be easy. Surely once she left Texas, she would have headed back to her hometown of Grazer's Corners.

Now he realized how foolish he'd been. The woman could have gone anywhere. For reasons he could only guess at, she'd witnessed a crime and fled, and for those same reasons, she wasn't likely to make herself easy to find.

Kate knew Mitch's name, which meant that, as he'd feared, the Gulch City police must have sent an All Points Bulletin to California. How long would it be before someone else in law enforcement spotted him and made the connection?

If he were to have any hope of securing his freedom permanently, Mitch needed help. And who better to help him than a sheriff? He settled his Stetson into place and jumped down. From here on out, he would have to trust Sheriff Kate with his life.

He could only hope he wouldn't live, or die, to regret it.

KATE WAS SURPRISED at how little the mangled state of her dress bothered her. It seemed like a temporary setback, nothing more.

A few days should give the town tailor a chance to replace her lace overskirt. Given her doubts about Moose, this delay might prove to be a good thing.

Once she figured out what to do about her uninvited guest, she and her fiancé would have time to talk about a lot of things they should have discussed earlier. That ought to ease her jittery nerves and get their marriage off to a better start.

With the newly exhumed key in hand, Kate replaced

the brick, crossed the porch and unlocked the back door. A sideways glance showed Mitch examining the rear of his truck, his finger tracing a bullet-sized ding in the bumper.

He hadn't driven away, even though she'd given him the chance. If he had, Kate supposed she would have called the CHP and let justice take its course.

But he'd stuck around, which meant there might to be more to this case than met the eye. Not that Mitch Connery didn't already present a striking eyeful.

Her body still hummed from their contact in the truck. Kate couldn't imagine traveling that way with Moose, even for a short time. He'd be making self-conscious jokes, while she would feel an overwhelming urge to push him away and regain her distance.

That was how she always reacted when Moose came close. Why hadn't she felt the same way with Mitch?

Functioning on automatic pilot, Kate plugged in the coffeemaker and retrieved two of her mother's lily-painted cups from the cabinet. She hadn't had time to pack up her household in the week since school ended, and anyway, she figured she'd have plenty of free time this summer to move slowly into Moose's place.

Mostly, it was hard to leave this home where she'd grown up. As she hurried into the master bedroom to change clothes, Kate could still smell her dad's after-shave lotion and her mom's perfume. The scents had seeped into the wood, becoming a permanent part of the house, like memories.

The wedding dress came off a lot more easily than it had gone on. With unaccustomed carelessness, Kate slapped it crookedly onto a hanger, tossed her slip and stockings on the bed and reached for a pair of jeans.

What was she thinking of? She was the sheriff, not a cowboy's date!

A pair of black slacks ought to do the trick. She couldn't resist adding a knit top trimmed in flowers, more feminine than her usual tailored look, but threw a black blazer over it and thrust her feet into low-heeled pumps.

Kate tossed away her flowered circlet and yanked a brush through her hair, scarcely glancing in the mirror. Okay, now she felt normal again.

A peek through the back window showed Mitch emerging from his camper. He must have gone in to check for damage.

She wondered what the inside of the camper looked like. It must be cramped, especially for a tall man. Did he keep everything neat and polished, or was he one of those guys who scarcely noticed grime on the floor and dirty dishes in the sink?

One thing was for sure, she mused as she returned to the kitchen. Mitch wouldn't have hired a trendy decorator, the way Moose had done when he bought his house.

Her gaze trailed over the flowers stenciled in a strip just below the ceiling. She'd helped her mother make that when she was, what, twelve years old?

Moose had called it old-fashioned. His tone had implied ''out of date.'' Perhaps he was right.

Kate reached down a bowl of sugar and a jar of artificial creamer. There was no milk, since she'd been planning to be gone a week on their honeymoon to Yosemite.

She grimaced. Somehow, camping in a tent hadn't been her idea of how to spend the first days of her marriage. She'd suggested Lake Tahoe, or perhaps even San Francisco, but Moose had vetoed those ideas as too expensive.

They really did need to talk about values, and about investing in their marriage. Maybe they didn't share quite as many views as Kate had assumed.

The door closed quietly when Mitch came into the kitchen. It was odd, but until now, she'd never realized that Moose always let it slam.

Mitch removed his hat. "It looks real homey in here."

"Kind of old-fashioned," Kate said apologetically.

"That's the best kind of fashion, in my book," replied the cowboy.

She had the illogical sense that the house approved of him. When other people came in—Moose in particular—the dimensions seemed to shrink and the lace curtains fluttered nervously.

Mitch's cedar scent blended right in. And he had a respectful way of crossing the wooden floor as lightly as if it were foam-cushioned. He didn't turn his chair and sit backwards in it as if he were visiting the Corner Bar, either. "I ought to call the church and let people know I'm okay." She poured the coffee into cups. "But first I need to hear your account."

"It will be the first time I've told it to anybody since the shooting." He set his hat on one of the chairs, crown-side down.

"You didn't talk to the Gulch City police?" She carried the cups to the table. "Don't you think that might have been better than running?"

"The chief is a close friend of Billy Parkinson's." Mitch's face took on an angry tightness. "Billy's the man who stole my parents' ranch, set me up to get killed and then hired this gang of cutthroats to finish the job.''

Kate wasn't sure she could absorb so much information in a single gulp. But one fact stood out. ''Then he's the man to blame for ruining my wedding.''

''I'm afraid that snake would consider it a plus,'' Mitch said. ''I've never seen a fellow with such plain cussedness, ma'am.''

''Do you think you could get used to saying Kate?'' she asked. ''Being called ma'am makes me feel like I'm ninety. They don't even call me that at my school.''

''Your school?''

''The kids call me Miss Bingham. The teachers call me Kate.'' She supposed this might be a good time to explain that she had no law-enforcement training. On the other hand, she *had* been elected, and Sneed Brockner was long gone. ''There's not much call for a full-time sheriff around here. At least, there didn't used to be.''

''You're the school principal?'' Some of the stiffness ebbed from his shoulders. ''Now, that I can see.''

''And a good one!'' She snapped the cream and sugar on the table. ''Do you cowboys use spoons, or just pour it in and stir with your finger?''

''Did I say something to rile you, ma'am?'' he drawled.

Kate didn't know why she felt so touchy. She loved working with the teachers and students, guiding her school toward excellence.

But somehow, in the past few days, she'd taken a liking to being called sheriff. Not that she intended to keep the job for long. But right now she held the responsibility, and she didn't want some tough guy assuming she couldn't handle a few gunslingers.

Handle gunslingers? Her, Kate Bingham? She plopped into her chair. "I must be suffering from delayed shock."

"That wouldn't surprise me." Almost shyly, Mitch extended one arm across the table and cradled her hand in his. "Ma'am, I mean, Kate, maybe I'm asking too much, but I don't know who else to turn to."

With her free hand, she lifted her cup and took a sip. "Let me see if I've got this straight. You're saying you were set up? How did that force you to break into a ranch house and shoot someone?"

"It's kind of a long story," the Texan admitted.

"Then you'd better let go of my hand. I might need it to take notes."

Releasing her, he sat back and stretched his legs onto the vacant chair, next to his hat. "Be my guest."

Kate reached into a shallow drawer her father had installed under the table, and removed a notepad and pen. "Shoot—I mean, go on."

"Billy Parkinson used to be my father's foreman, but he started drinking and backtalking, so Dad fired him," Mitch said. "I was the one who physically threw him off the ranch, and he swore to get even."

Kate realized she ought to probe for inconsistencies. "If he's such a lowlife, how did he come to be friends with the police chief?"

"They're both from Rio Saba. That's a town even smaller than Gulch City," Mitch explained.

"Old friends?" Coming from a small town herself, she could understand the tie.

He nodded. "From their high school days. Anyway, Mom died when I was in college, and about ten years ago, Daddy went too. That's when Billy showed up with papers signed by my father, making the ranch collateral on a loan."

"A loan?" Kate was writing as fast as she could. She hoped she'd be able to read her scrawl later.

"Dad had borrowed some money many years earlier, during a drought," Mitch said. "It was from a friend of his, the town doctor. I'm sure Dad repaid it, but there weren't any receipts to prove it and the doctor had retired to Arizona, then died a couple of years before Dad did."

The ballpoint pen left a blue smear on Kate's index finger, which she ignored. "So, how did Billy Parkinson come by the papers? And how could he prove he'd taken over the loan?"

"He said he'd gone to Arizona and bought it because—so he claimed—Dad had stopped making payments. He had a quitclaim supposedly signed by Doc Rosen, whose signature looked like a jagged scrawl. I hired a handwriting expert, who said it might be a forgery, but he couldn't be sure."

"Why didn't Billy demand payment while your Dad was still alive?"

"He claimed he wanted revenge on me, which is believable enough. But I think he somehow got the loan papers from the doctor's estate and forged the quitclaim," Mitch explained.

"Surely someone in the doctor's family would know how he got the papers," Kate pressed.

"His daughter's been out of the country. I haven't been able to reach her." Mitch gripped the edge of the table. "Kate, you have to understand. I was twenty-five years old, not long out of college, and grieving for my father. I had no expertise in dealing with finances, no money for lawyers, and no friends in high places.''

"And this man Parkinson had his buddy the police chief," she filled in.

She could read the rest in his tortured gaze. "They threw me off my ranch. I love that place, Kate. It's called the High C—my grandfather named it in Grandma's honor, because she used to be a singer. He built the house with his own hands. I meant to live my whole life there."

No wonder he appreciated her old-fashioned kitchen, she reflected with a wrench of sympathy. "You must have tried to get it back."

"I did everything I could think of, everything legal," Mitch said. "I felt like I'd betrayed my own family, letting it go that way. I didn't have enough money to pay a lawyer for a long court battle, and that made me mad."

Understanding dawned. "So you went to law school yourself."

"If you can't lick 'em, join 'em." Mitch shrugged. "I guess Billy Parkinson figured I was gone for good when I left Gulch City. He couldn't have been happy when I came back and hung my shingle. And especially when I filed my own lawsuit."

So far, Kate was strongly on Mitch's side. She supposed the whole story could be invented, but the APB *did* list him as an attorney. "So, who was Jules Kominsky and how did you come to shoot him?"

Mitch seemed absorbed in staring at one of his boots. "Excuse me, but do you have any leather polish?"

"Are you joking?" she asked.

"Ma'am... Kate, a cowboy always takes care of his

equipment, and there's nothing more important than his boots.'' Mitch swung his legs to the floor. ''I'm afraid I've let things go this past week.''

''Is this some kind of delaying tactic?'' she asked.

A startled expression crossed his face. ''Maybe so. I'd forgotten how good it feels, sitting in a kitchen in a woman's house, with lace curtains at the windows and those pretty stenciled flowers around the wall. Reminds me of home, the home I don't have anymore.''

Kate's memory flashed back to the time a fourth-grader got sent to her office as a habitual trouble-maker. In the course of half an hour of talking, all the bluster had peeled away and she'd found herself facing a lonely little boy in desperate need of attention.

She'd been able to help him with the cooperation of his mother and the Big Brothers program. Mitch wasn't going to be so easy to rescue, but she found herself wanting very much to try.

A real sheriff would never react this way, Kate told herself as she found some leather cleaner and rags under the sink. *On the other hand, this isn't exactly a hardened criminal you're dealing with here, either.*

In fact, there was something endearingly domestic about Mitch as, with apologies, he covered a chair with newspaper, removed his boots and began spreading polish on them. Moose got his shoes polished by a man who worked at the car wash, and she had a suspicion he didn't tip very well, either.

She must stop having negative thoughts about Moose, Kate scolded herself. Everybody had annoying habits, including her.

Mitch resumed talking as he buffed. ''Last week, Billy asked me to meet him at the ranch to discuss a settlement. I didn't believe any good would come of it, but civil cases can drag on for years, so I figured I should hear him out.''

"And this Kominsky fellow tried to shoot you?" She realized she was leading the witness. "I mean, what happened then?"

"When I got there, the house was lit up but nobody answered the bell," Mitch replied. "There was a note that said they were downstairs watching TV and just to come on in. So I did."

Kate scribbled some more. She was running out of paper.

"You can guess the rest." He rubbed hard on one patch of heel, scraping away a speck of dirt so small Kate couldn't see it. "I called out, but no one replied. When I reached the hall, Jules fired at me. I dodged and he missed, so I shot back."

"You brought a gun?" she asked.

"I'd have been a fool not to." Mitch frowned at his boot. "Durn. I think the leather's nicked."

"Did you hit him?"

"Not the first time. I shouted at him to put his gun down," he said. "His words, and I heard them quite clearly, were, 'Not for what Billy's paying me.'"

"'Not for what Billy's paying me,'" she repeated in disgust, and wrote it down.

"I didn't want to shoot him, Kate. I didn't like him much, and I especially didn't like him living on my ranch, but I never killed a man before and I wish I could have avoided it this time."

"He fired again?" she asked.

"Twice. I had nowhere to turn in that hallway, no choice but to shoot back," Mitch said. "I could hear people coming up from the basement just as he got hit, and I figured they had guns too, so I ran."

Then, she gathered, Mitch fled Gulch City with Billy's gang after him and a biased police chief waiting to railroad him. It all tracked, except for one point.

"So, just naturally you drove halfway across the country to Grazer's Corners, well-known haven for escaped murderers, and hid out at my wedding in full view of no more than a couple of hundred people," Kate said. "Very sensible."

His mouth twisted. "It does sound odd. You see, my only chance of clearing my name is to produce a witness who can verify what really happened."

He couldn't possibly think one of those bandits was going to vouch for him. "There was someone else at the ranch?" she asked.

Mitch began working on the second boot. "My cousin, Loretta. She loved that place and blamed me for losing it, so she'd gone to work as Billy's secretary. She didn't exactly see what happened that night, but she must have heard something to indicate they were expecting me, that I didn't just break in. Without her, I don't have a defense."

"You thought she might come here?" Kate set aside the notebook, which was full. Besides, they seemed to have reached the end of the story.

"She grew up in Grazer's Corners," Mitch said. "Loretta Blaine. You wouldn't happen to know her, would you?"

Of course she did, at least slightly. Loretta was half a dozen years younger than Kate, but it would be hard not to recognize the woman with the most beautiful voice in the history of the church choir.

"I headed a drive to raise a scholarship so she could finish her last year at the music conservatory," Kate said. "She's your cousin?"

"The only one I've got. We're a small family." He finished burnishing the boots to a dazzling shine. "I think maybe she got scared when she saw how violent Billy's boys could get. I was hoping she'd come back here and maybe turn up at church."

"I haven't seen her in ages," Kate said.

"It was just bad timing, about your wedding." With loving care, Mitch inspected the leather. "It was my intent to drop by the Sunday service, but when I called to find out the time, the pastor said there was a wedding on Saturday and invited me."

"The whole town was invited," Kate said.

"That's how it ought to be," Mitch said. "Doesn't seem like people do things that way much anymore."

He pulled on the boots and sat regarding her. Silence lengthened, broken only by the ticking of the grandfather clock in the hall.

Finally he said, "These rags are pretty dirty. I can run a load of wash if you like."

Kate couldn't believe it. A man described as armed and dangerous was offering to do laundry rather than leave a few soiled cloths behind. "Thanks, but that would take too long. Just keep them or toss them."

"I guess that means you want me to leave, huh?" he said.

Judging by the way his jaw was twitching, Kate gathered he wanted to say more. "What else?" she said.

"What else what?"

"What else were you going to say?"

"I always figured teachers were mind readers," Mitch said. "I guess principals are even worse."

"We try," said Kate.

"I'd like you to come with me." Mitch held his

gaze steady, boring into hers. "Loretta's obviously in a panic. Seeing you might at least calm her down long enough to talk to me."

"I'm the sheriff," Kate said. "It's bad enough if I let you go. I certainly can't go with you."

"Consider it an investigation." For the first time, she could see a hint of lawyerlike caginess in his argument. "You'd be solving a crime."

"Texas isn't my jurisdiction," she said.

"You've had a bunch of bad guys shoot up the church here in Grazer's Corners," Mitch argued. "That *is* your jurisdiction."

"And having a woman along would make you a lot less conspicuous," Kate guessed. "Not to mention the practical advantages of traveling with your own personal sheriff. I'm sorry to disillusion you, Mitch, but I don't even have a badge yet, let alone know how to shoot a gun. I just got elected."

His mouth curved into a boyish smile. "Then consider it an adventure. I'm guessing that you could use one before you settle down with—what's his name?"

"Oh, my goodness, Moose!" Kate jumped up and flew to the wall phone. "He must be crazy with worry!"

"Your fiancé is named Moose?" Mitch asked.

She started to point out that it was a nickname, then decided she didn't want to hear whatever comments he would make about the name *Bledsoe*. Instead, she pushed the rapid-dial button for Moose's cellular phone.

His familiar tenor answered on the second ring. "Harmon here."

"Moose? It's me!"

"Kate! What's that animal done to you?"

"Excuse me?" she said.

"Jeanie Jeffrey told us about the All Points Bulletin. Has that monster, has he, well...has he?"

"Has he what?" Then it hit her. "Moose Harmon! First of all, that man saved my life! Second, I barely escaped a hail of bullets, and you're worried that he might have compromised my virtue? I can't believe it!"

"Well, that sort of man, you never know what he'll do," Moose snorted. "And I've waited a long time for this."

She could feel steam shooting from her ears. "I'm all in one piece, thank you *very* much."

"Where are you? Is he gone?" Moose demanded.

Kate was in no mood to be interrogated. "This man has been framed for a crime he didn't...didn't exactly commit. Since, thanks to you, I happen to be the sheriff here, I'll handle things my way."

"Handle things?" he said. "This isn't some boy accused of throwing spit wads in class. I'll take over now, Kate."

"You'll *what?*" She couldn't believe his nerve. "Excuse me, when did you get elected to be the law around here?"

"I'm calling in the authorities," growled Moose. "Whether you like it or not."

"I *am* the authorities," she cried before she could stop herself, "and if you go over my head, Moose Harmon, I will never ever walk down the aisle with you as long as I live, and you can wait for you-know-what until your...your ego falls off!"

"But Kate—"

"And for your information, I've got an attorney assisting me on this investigation," she snapped. "So you pipe down and hang tight, and I'll be back when I'm back!''

She slammed the phone into its cradle. It was the first time Kate had ever hung up on anyone.

''Need help packing?'' asked the cowboy, an amused gleam in his eye.

''I'm already packed,'' said Kate, and went to get her suitcase.

Chapter Four

"I can't believe I'm doing this." They were swinging north around the town through an almond orchard. It was a roundabout route to the freeway, but Kate still feared Moose might alert the CHP to watch for them.

It would be the ultimate humiliation for the sheriff of Grazer's Corners to get pulled over and taken into custody in her own bailiwick. If that happened, she would spend the rest of her life devising ways to make Moose miserable.

But he hadn't actually done anything wrong yet, so why was she angry with him? She had never imagined she could feel so mixed up and fluttery and snappish and embarrassed, all at once.

This wasn't the rock-steady Kate Bingham she'd known for thirty-one years. But she had a good idea what the problem might be.

Today was supposed to be her wedding day, and tonight her wedding night. She'd been looking forward to this event for nearly half her life.

Then something had gone wrong. The strangest part was that she felt suffused with a sense of relief.

Brides and grooms often got cold feet, or so she'd heard. Maybe that explained why, instead of returning to the church, she had grabbed her suitcase and piled into the pickup with Mitch.

Kate hadn't been able to bring herself to consider the consequences, and darn it, she still couldn't. "Did you slip something into my coffee? I don't feel like myself."

At the wheel, Mitch rolled his window down partway. "Don't blame me, Miss Kate. It was that boyfriend of yours who got your dander up."

"He can be annoying," she agreed. "But he's a good man, underneath."

"He must be, if you love him," said her companion.

"Do you always say the right thing?" she asked.

"I'm a lawyer." A fly blew in through the open window. He squinted at it assessingly.

"They teach you diplomacy in law school?"

"No. They teach you survival, by default." With a smooth unhurried gesture, Mitch batted the fly back outside. "You either figure out the unwritten rules and snow the heck out of your teachers, or they bounce you. Most law school flunkouts don't have a clue where they went wrong."

"It sounds horrible," Kate said.

"There's a certain satisfaction when you make it." Mitch rolled up the window. "But I don't guess you come out in a real friendly mood."

They reached a crossroads, and Kate pointed left, away from the mountains. "I guess we'd better start angling toward the freeway. Of course, that depends on where we're going."

Mitch tipped back his Stetson but didn't respond. Around them, the almond groves yielded to vineyards. Overhead, a hawk circled lazily, and she wondered whether some hapless rabbit had made the mistake of venturing from its burrow.

"Where *are* we going?" Kate pressed. She wished she knew how to conduct an investigation, and then it occurred to her that the proper technique would probably involve an office, a computer, a fax machine and a telephone.

Not riding in a truck through the countryside. Not keeping company with a fugitive. Not making sideways glances at a tanned face and a taut physique, and wishing his belt buckle would sneak up on her again.

"I've been giving it some thought," Mitch said at last.

The hawk circled a few more times and flew away. The shadow of a distant barn lengthened in the afternoon sunlight, and Kate discovered she was hungry.

"What exactly have you thought up?" she asked.

"There's three things we have to do." He flipped down his sunshade as the road curved and the lowering sun hit their eyes dead-on. "First, avoid cops. Second, avoid Tiny Wheeler and his gang."

"Tiny Wheeler?" she said. "That would be the big hulking one?"

Mitch nodded. "The fellow who limps, he's called Nine Toes Blankenship. And the kid, he's Dexter Dinkens. Eager but not notoriously bright."

"I guess the number three thing we have to do is to find Loretta," Kate said.

"Yep." Mitch tapped his thumb against the steering wheel as if keeping rhythm to music that she couldn't hear. "You know her, right? Any idea where she might go?"

Kate pictured the young woman as she'd looked a year and a half ago when she soloed in the church

Christmas concert. Curly brown hair tumbling to her shoulders, olive-colored eyes wide and full of enthusiasm.

"She loves music," Kate recalled. "It's the only thing I really know about her."

"My whole family's musical," Mitch said.

"Singing cowboys?"

He laughed. "Not exactly. My grandmother Luisa was an opera singer over in Europe. She was on tour in Dallas when she met Grandpa. The story is, he went all the way to Italy to win her hand."

"I'm surprised she would leave her homeland. Especially for a man she couldn't have known very well."

It occurred to Kate that Mich had induced *her* to abandon, at least temporarily, her town and her fiancé. But she doubted Mitch's grandfather had rescued Luisa from gunslingers.

"She used to tease that it was because she saw World War II coming," Mitch said. "But anyone could see they were crazy in love. My Aunt Micaela, Loretta's mom, inherited Grandma's beautiful voice. She chose not to make a career of it, though."

"What about you?" Kate asked. "Do you sing?"

They were passing a cotton field. "Not in public," Mitch replied.

"This isn't public," she couldn't resist saying.

"It's more public than the shower."

She decided not to argue. "Let's get back to your cousin. She couldn't have been at the ranch long. As I recall, she just finished music school in January."

"She'd only been there a few months," he agreed. "It's possible that when she fled, she headed back to the conservatory to see her friends. Any idea where it is?''

''It's called the Sungold Hills Academy of Music,'' Kate said. ''That's in Pasadena, just north of downtown L.A. But how can you be sure she's not still in Texas?''

''It's my home state, not hers. Her only tie is to the High C—she used to spend summers with us,'' he explained. ''I can't see why she'd stay in a state where she doesn't know anyone. I don't suppose you know who any of her friends are, do you?''

''At the scholarship luncheon, she brought a guy along, although I don't think they were romantically involved,'' Kate recalled. ''They sang a duet from *La Bohème*.''

''Do you remember his name?''

''It sounded German,'' she said. ''Horst, I think. Horst Gewurst or Gewitt, or Wittstein, or... Wittgenstein, that was it.''

She was amazed that she remembered. Now that she concentrated, she could even picture him, a slim fellow with a mop of black hair overpowering his face.

They were approaching Highway 99. If anyone were on the lookout for them, this would be the place they'd get stopped.

Kate scanned the area. A truck pulling a horse carrier lumbered along a crossroad. A blue sedan sat on the shoulder, but she couldn't see who was inside. Might it be an undercover unit?

As they passed, she looked straight down and saw a road map open on the driver's lap. Just a traveler, checking his route.

Mitch swung up a ramp onto the freeway. ''Keep your eyes peeled for that van. I figure Tiny's gang knows where Loretta went to school, too. They may not have any brains but Billy does, and he's probably directing them by phone.''

It frightened her to think of what Billy's ruffians might do if they found Loretta before Mitch did. The young woman had radiated confidence at the luncheon, but she would be no match for a bunch of gunslingers.

''I'll go as far as Pasadena with you,'' Kate said. ''You might have a better chance of finding your cousin with me along.''

Mitch gave her one of his unreadable glances. ''I'm grateful. I hate to point it out, since I do need your help, but you sure are stirring up a mess of trouble for yourself.''

''I don't see it that way,'' she answered. ''These hoodlums shot up my town and wrecked my wedding. They're also a threat to Loretta. I want them brought back to face charges.''

He crooked her an admiring grin. ''You are one tough hombre, Madam Principal.''

''That's what all the kids say.'' She managed a smile in return.

At the same time, her own words surprised Kate. Who was this woman who couldn't wait to bring bad guys to justice and who relished the wind in her hair? Well, maybe just a slight draft through the side vent, but the point was that she felt in no hurry to return to Grazer's Corners or to Moose.

It struck her that she hadn't had a real vacation since high school, one in which she didn't have to answer to or be responsible for anybody. She'd always taken pride in her dedication, without considering that maybe she needed a break.

On a honeymoon with Moose, she would have instinctively catered to his needs and tastes. Mitch was different. He didn't belong to her, nor she to him.

If he wanted to eat hamburgers every day, that didn't mean she had to. If he annoyed her, she could tell him to chill out.

For once in her life, Kate could simply be herself. It was a wonderful feeling.

It would have been even more wonderful without the hunger pangs. "I hate to mention it, but what are we going to do for dinner?"

"There's a granola bar in the glove box," Mitch said. "If you can hold out for a couple of hours, I'll find us a place to camp near Fresno. Then we can cook something decent."

"Right." Kate fished out the granola bar, split it in half and gave Mitch his share. It wasn't much to eat, but in her years as a teacher and a principal, she had often skipped meals.

She settled back, chewing the sticky bar slowly and hoping she hadn't forgotten to pack her toothbrush. At least, thanks to Moose's rustic idea of a honeymoon, she'd brought appropriate clothes for camping.

It made sense to stop en route. The drive to Pasadena could take seven or eight hours, especially since they didn't dare speed. And there was nothing to be gained by arriving in the middle of the night.

The middle of the night. Just exactly what *were* the sleeping arrangements going to be in that tiny camper perched on the back of the pickup?

Kate decided to worry about it when the time came.

THE TOWN COUNCIL held an informal meeting around a chipped fake-marble table at the Good Eats Diner. Moose knew that secret sessions were illegal in California, but since half the town had crowded in to join them, he didn't see a problem.

Razz Fiddle, his long hippie hair pulled back with a rubber band, wielded two carafes of coffee, both leaded. Even so, he was having a hard time keeping up with this bunch.

"I can't believe you haven't called the FBI!" Maynard Grazer was roaring. "My daughter's getting married in that church next Saturday. What if somebody kidnaps *her?*"

Moose spread his hands appeasingly. "I'm telling you, Kate went of her own free will. She wants to crack this case. You know her. Once she gets an idea in her head, she runs with it."

"I could send a bulletin," Jeanie Jeffrey offered from the sidelines. "I've always wanted to send out an APB."

"I appreciate your concern, but it's not necessary." Moose tried not to let the others see him squirm. If Jeanie or anybody else jumped the gun, Kate would never believe it hadn't been his idea.

Small towns like this didn't produce many women worthy of Moose Harmon. If he lost her, where was he going to find another one?

"I'm in agreement with Moose." To his surprise, the comment came from Randall Latrobe, Jordan Grazer's fiancé. The young banker was suave, successful and a little too pretty for Moose's taste. He was also not known for disagreeing with his future father-in-law. "Maynard, I believe there may be one aspect you haven't considered."

"And what would that be?" demanded the town's patriarch.

"Bad publicity. Call the FBI and we could bring the big-city media down on top of us."

"So?" said Ned Grand, who alternated turns on the town council with his brother Moe. "The bakery could use the business."

"Shoot-outs in the town square? Even in the church?" Randall's voice never wavered from its almost hypnotic evenness. "Just imagine what that image could do to real estate prices."

Maynard grunted a reluctant concession. Moose felt some of the tension ease from his gut.

"What I can't believe," spoke up Charity Arden, who was perched atop the corner of Jeanie's table, "is that you people aren't more worried about Kate."

Now that Maynard had backed off, reassuring words came easily to Moose. "I have the utmost respect for her judgment. If my woman feels this is the best way to handle the situation, I think we ought to let her do it."

"Your woman?" repeated Charity in disbelief.

"The woman I love," boomed Moose, who liked the sound of the phrase.

Maynard Grazer tapped his fingers irritably on the table. "I must admit, Kate Bingham is a capable female. That's why I supported her for school principal, and voted for her for sheriff. Didn't the rest of you?"

Around the room, heads nodded.

"Then let's let her do her job," said Randall with a satisfied smile.

"Well," said a dry voice. "I suppose she can handle the situation, but can she handle *him?*"

Everyone's gaze fixed on Agatha Flintstone, who sat with the council members. "What do you mean?" asked Moose.

"How could anyone not notice?" sighed the crusty lady, fluffing her beehive hairdo. "That man swept her into his arms like a knight from the Middle Ages. All he lacked was the armor, and in a pinch we can dispense with that."

"Oh, spare us," grumbled Moose.

"Mark my words," said Agatha, "sooner or later she's going to ask herself if you measure up. Do you, Mr. Mayor?"

Maynard waved aside her comments impatiently. "I think we'd best keep out of Moose's private business, Agatha. Randall's raised a good point, and I agree we should all sit tight and trust in Kate's judgment."

"Typical," muttered Charity as she jumped off the table and marched out the door.

People began wandering away after that, somewhat to Moose's disappointment. Council meetings didn't often draw this kind of attendance.

He was the last of the officials to leave. From a booth where he hadn't noticed her, Betsy Muller came to join him.

Moose hoped she wasn't going to ask for a raise. Betsy did a good job selling makeup but a little too much of the stock ended up on her face.

"Moose?" she said in her quavery voice. "Wow, you were amazing."

"I was?" He frowned. "In what way?"

"The way you...dominated everybody." She stared up at him with pale eyes rimmed in Cleopatra black. "I think it's just awful, Kate going off and leaving you on your wedding day. And wedding night."

A man couldn't miss the hint, especially since, as people had observed to Moose over the years, Betsy had an awful crush on him.

"Well, thanks," he said. "But she'll be back soon. Maybe tomorrow."

The young woman nibbled on a strand of dyed-platinum hair, then pushed it away with her tongue. "If you were my fellow, I wouldn't leave you for a minute."

To Moose's surprise, her words felt like balm on his injured pride. "Really?"

"I wouldn't risk letting some other woman get close to you." She took a step toward him, absent-mindedly pushing a bra strap into place beneath her almost-sheer blouse. At this angle, Moose noticed that Betsy's figure was more filled out than he'd realized, or maybe she was just moving in a particularly alluring way tonight.

Tonight. His wedding night. And after all these years of waiting, he would be going home alone. It didn't seem fair.

"You ought to be careful," he said. "A fellow might, er, misinterpret your sympathy."

"No, he wouldn't," said Betsy.

Moose knew he should tell this young woman to clear off, but the words got stuck in his throat. "Uh…" was all that came out.

She was practically pressed against him now, those ultrathick lashes fluttering like eager butterflies. "Hey, honey bear. Can I call you that? I've always thought of you as a honey bear."

"You can call him anything you like," said Razz Fiddle in a voice so flat it bordered on irony. "But you and your honey bear need to hibernate somewhere else. The café is closed."

With a start, Moose realized how this must look. His wedding had been interrupted and his bride stolen, and now the head of his cosmetics department was applying herself to him in a public place. It was not the sort of behavior a town like Grazer's Corner's expected from its mayor.

"Time for you to go home, Betsy." He caught her by the shoulders and steered her out the door. "And me, too. Alone."

"But Moose," she started to protest, then caught his quelling look. "I mean, uh, Mr. Harmon. Couldn't we talk about this someplace private?"

"I'll see you at work on Monday," he said, and headed for his car without looking back.

Kate had better return soon, he reflected grimly. She had just better.

A FEW MILES from Fresno, Mitch located the rough-and-ready campground he was seeking, the kind with no hookups, no overnight fees, few other campers and no nosy rangers.

He halted the pickup on a rutted dirt turnout in a woebegone clump of trees. Most of the other campsites stood vacant, although he glimpsed the metallic gleam of a trailer some distance away.

Through the windshield, Kate regarded the splintered picnic table assessingly. "I suppose we could do something with that," she said. "Do you have one of those indestructible tablecloths, the kind you could rig as a ship's sail in a pinch?"

"Why?" he asked. "You expecting a flood?"

She flicked some lint off her tailored black jacket. "Just making it clear that I'm not looking for linen and lace, thank you."

"I've got one somewhere." Mitch opened his door. "Eating out isn't a bad idea. You may not have noticed, but there's nowhere to recharge, so we do need to conserve electricity.''

"I'll cancel the midnight film festival on the VCR, then,'' Kate returned, and thumped to earth on her side of the truck.

When she came around to meet him in back, Mitch was startled to notice how small she was. Not that he hadn't had ample time to take Kate's measure before, but she just didn't have a short personality.

In fact, she reminded him in some ways of one of his professors at law school. The woman had always stayed several steps ahead of even her quickest-witted student, and let everyone know it. He knew some men didn't like being bested by a woman, but Mitch enjoyed a good battle of wits.

The only problem in Kate's case lay in the fact that he had a clear sensual recollection of the enticing curves that lay beneath that businesslike jacket. As a result, their verbal fencing felt like a prelude to physical intimacy.

But he could see from her expression that she wasn't flirting with him. He stepped aside and let her climb the two steps into the camper's interior.

As always, the scent of his hand-crafted cedar cabinets wafted out. "There's a switch to your right,'' he called.

Inside, a bulb clicked on. "This is impressive.'' Kate's voice floated back. "It's completely equipped. And bigger than it looks.''

"The bathroom's small.'' Mitch stayed outside, knowing how tight the quarters were. Especially for two people who shouldn't touch each other.

"Yes, but it's *got* a bathroom, which is what counts.'' From the sound of it, she might have been evaluating a new portable classroom for her school. "And everything's spotless. Even the stove." There was a pause. "I see where you sleep, on top of the cab. That's the only bed?"

"The table folds away and the couch opens," he said. "But it's warm enough that I think I'll sleep outside tonight."

He heard the click of a latch and knew she must be checking the cabinets. "Plenty of food," she observed. "How does spaghetti sound?"

"Is any part of your family Italian?" asked Mitch.

"Not that I know of."

"I'm sorry, but you're not allowed near the pasta pot," he declared.

A pair of slightly dusty pumps appeared on the steps. Two trim pants legs, hiked slightly to reveal slender ankles, descended until Kate plunked herself down the last drop to the ground.

In the twilight, her blue eyes challenged him. "You can cook if you like," she returned, "but my mother taught me how to make spaghetti and no one's ever complained."

Mitch supposed he shouldn't be so picky, but he'd spent too much of his life eating overcooked pasta, in restaurants and sometimes private homes. "Do you know the meaning of the phrase *al dente?*"

"Why don't you just get in there and demonstrate it, like a real man?" she teased. "And hand down my tote bag while you're at it."

The woman was certainly not shy about giving orders. Mitch was beginning to see why Moose had left Kate in the middle of the street to fend for herself.

Then he remembered the way the groom had nearly bowled over the minister en route to his escape, and was finally forced to take the elderly man with him. Maybe the lady had developed her crusty manners in self-defense.

Besides, Mitch was too hungry to think straight. He handed down the tote, a tablecloth and dinnerware, then ran cold water into the pasta pot. He was glad he'd refilled the camper's tank that morning.

Dinner was nothing to brag about, just canned corn and pasta with sauce from a jar, but Mitch was surprised at how good it smelled as he carried the pots down to the table. He was also surprised at how much he looked forward to sharing the meal, after spending so many nights alone.

Having set the table, Kate sat on one of the benches reading a magazine by flashlight. She had put on a pair of glasses that made her eyes look even larger than usual.

"What are you reading?" Mitch said as he dished out the spaghetti.

"An educational journal."

She'd packed a professional publication to take on her honeymoon?

"I try to keep up," Kate continued, tucking the periodical into her bag. "There never seems to be enough time."

Never enough time. The phrase echoed through Mitch's mind.

There had never been enough time for him, either, he realized. At thirty-five, he felt as if his adult life had whizzed past. Intent on regaining the ranch, he hadn't even given a thought to finding a wife or starting a family the way most men did.

Maybe that was why he felt so unreasonably glad

to have her company at the table. Men, he supposed, had nesting instincts, too.

Kate tucked a napkin into her collar bib-style and tackled the spaghetti. After neatly downing the first bite, she said, "So this is what they mean by *al dente*. It's just barely done. Not gummy at all."

"My grandmother had very high standards. So do I."

"The sauce is good," Kate acknowledged. "Bottled?"

He gave a short nod. "Doctored with a little garlic powder and a dash of basil. Some oregano. Maybe a pinch of parsley."

"'Fess up," she said. "There's sherry in here."

He chuckled. "You're stealing my family secrets."

"If we'd planned ahead, we could have brought fresh herbs from my garden," Kate mused.

"Green thumb?"

"I mostly stick plants in the ground and let them fend for themselves, but they do okay." She finished her corn and set down her fork. "Now," she stated, "we need a plan for tomorrow."

Wasn't this carrying organization to extremes? "Basically, I thought we'd drive to Pasadena and see if we can locate this Wittgenstein character," Mitch said.

"And tell him what?" Kate pressed. "That you're a notorious murderer who would like to force your cousin to testify on your behalf? That should impress him."

He hated to admit it, but she had a point. "What would you suggest?"

"First of all, it's possible we'll actually run into

Loretta,'' she replied. ''Do you think she'd talk to you?''

He kept getting an image of Loretta when she was ten years old, a freckled kid with curly hair who'd followed him around the ranch all summer. ''She used to look up to me. But I guess that ended when I lost the High C.''

''Why?'' The moon had come out, and in its glow Kate's face took on a cool watchfulness.

''I don't know,'' he admitted. ''I guess she sort of blamed me.''

''Did you explain to her what happened with Billy Parkinson and the loan? And how hard you were working to get the ranch back?''

He reflected for a moment. ''No. What happened was, I dropped her father a note. My aunt had died the summer before, and my uncle and I didn't keep in real close contact. Loretta was only fifteen, and it never occurred to me to talk to her personally.''

''Where's your uncle now?'' Kate asked.

''Japan. He works for a multinational company,'' Mitch said. ''I called him a few days ago, but he hadn't heard from his daughter.''

''Wasn't he worried?''

''He's not the worrying kind.'' Mitch's uncle Bert had a placid outlook on life. With him, it was out of sight, out of mind. ''The women in our family are mostly like Grandma Luisa, kind of excitable. My aunt was, for sure. But they tend to marry easygoing men.''

''Well, whether we find Loretta tomorrow or not, I think I should be the one to make the approach,'' Kate said.

This was Mitch's problem, and his family. ''I can handle this myself.''

"Oh?" From the way her eyebrows lifted and she pushed her glasses higher on her nose, he could have sworn she really was his law professor and he'd just given the wrong answer. "And what will you do when someone runs screaming for the telephone and calls out the SWAT team?"

Mitch had to admit he was fighting the inevitable. "Now that you mention it," he admitted, "you have a point."

"We'll make contact together. My presence may reassure Loretta, and if we find just Horst, he might remember me from the luncheon," Kate said. "I made the scholarship presentation."

And a music academy was more comfortable territory for a school principal than for a cowboy, even one with a law degree, Mitch thought ruefully. "Thanks. But I don't want to impose on you too much."

"Don't worry." She collected their empty paper plates and tossed them into a trash receptacle. "I'm just trying to bring those bandits to justice while they're still near my jurisdiction. If they're long gone, I'll take a bus back to Grazer's Corners tomorrow."

"Fair enough." He tried to erase any hint of regret from his voice. "We should make an early night of it, then."

A glint of moonlight caught her a glancing blow, or perhaps he simply hadn't noticed her wistful expression before. Tonight, Mitch recalled, was supposed to be her wedding night.

With that lumbering oaf, Moose! But, he reminded himself, he ought to show more respect for Kate's judgment. The man must have qualities that weren't immediately apparent.

Wrapped in thought, Mitch carried the pots inside. Maybe Moose did know something. At least he was willing to trust Kate to do things her own way.

Mitch was having a hard time letting her take the lead but, at least as far as tomorrow was concerned, he knew he should trust her.

He'd always been a loner, intent on solving his problems himself. He hadn't asked for any help from Uncle Bert, and it had never occurred to him to consult Loretta about his plans to regain the High C.

If he had, maybe she wouldn't have gone to work for Billy Parkinson. She must have had some ulterior motive, since secretarial work wasn't her career interest.

He wished he were the sort of person his cousin had felt she could confide in. But to achieve that, he would have had to open up to her first.

As he scrubbed the pots, Mitch reflected that he had never considered the value of letting others see his vulnerabilities. How ironic that he was learning this lesson from Kate, who belonged to another man.

Tomorrow, they would try their best to function as a team. Then they would go their separate ways.

That was fine with him. Until he got this mess cleared up and reclaimed the ranch, he was better off working alone.

Chapter Five

Kate awoke to the scent of cedar and a lingering, subliminal essence that clung to the sheets and pillowcase. The effect was so fundamentally masculine that she felt as if she had lain all night in a man's arms.

For one confused moment, she felt a spurt of joy. It was the morning after her wedding night, and somehow the magic must have happened. A sense of well-being mixed with excitement prickled through her body, and she prepared to nestle against her husband.

But when she rolled onto her side, there was no warm body beside her. Besides, surely this pleasurable ache ought to be accompanied by a dazzling awareness of how it felt to make love.

Then she blinked her eyes open. From where she lay on a shelflike bed overlooking the interior of the camper, she could see that it was definitely not home. Neither hers, nor Moose's.

She felt a twinge of disappointment, followed by embarrassment. Of course she hadn't had a wedding night, because she hadn't completed her wedding.

Images flooded her brain: Bandits. Shots whizzing through the church. Moose scampering for cover. Charity throwing a film can.

Somehow, in the course of one day, the world had tilted. Nothing was the same, and she wasn't sure it ever could be again.

Kate didn't exactly regret coming on this trip. She just wished she could get back to feeling like her old self.

She groped for her glasses and was adjusting them into place when, at the far end of the camper, the door opened. A well-shaped silhouette appeared in a wash of sunlight.

"Morning." Mitch angled inside and through the narrow path between the walled-off bathroom and the stove. With his hair slicked back and his face freshly washed, he looked remarkably cheerful for having spent the night sleeping on hard ground. "Care for breakfast?"

"Where did you clean up?" Kate asked.

"There's a stream down the road a piece. Is that your way of saying hello?"

"I'm grumpy in the morning." Her parents had given her a wide berth upon arising, and she had assumed a husband would soon learn to do the same. But Mitch wasn't her husband. "Excuse my manners. How are you?"

"Hungry," he said. "Frozen waffles okay?"

"You've got a microwave?"

"Toaster oven." He set to work, humming a tune she couldn't catch. Kate was impressed by the grace with which the tall man moved through the confined area.

She doubted she would be very graceful herself when she tried to squeeze past him to the bathroom. There was another problem as well: while most of the items in her suitcase were of the rough-and-ready variety, the same could not be said for her nightgown.

Left to her own devices, Kate would have taken one of her usual flannel gowns. But, in anticipation of his wedding night, Moose, who had an entire department store at his disposal, had presented her with a diaphanous concoction trimmed in black lace that hid only the most strategic points.

In Kate's opinion, it had been unsuitable for a tent. It was even more unsuitable to wear while scooting through a camper in front of a total stranger.

"Cover your eyes," she said.

At the counter, Mitch turned from preparing breakfast to stare at her. "Why?"

"Just pretend you're a gentleman, and do as I ask."

His jaw worked as if he wanted to argue. Kate was in no mood to debate the issue, so she snatched a change of clothes from her suitcase and threw back the covers.

Mitch's eyes widened and one of his hands jerked against the hot toaster oven. He snatched it back with a curse, followed by a muttered apology.

"Next time, listen to me," Kate snapped as she marched toward the bathroom. Mitch moved out of her way so fast, she might have been made of acid.

Changing clothes inside the tiny chamber was like trying on a bathing suit. Kate tugged and wiggled and squirmed, trying to get the nightgown off and her jeans on without banging into the sink. Next time, she was going to throw the man out of the camper entirely so she had enough space.

She didn't understand why fellows made such a big deal about women's bodies, anyway. Moose always seemed to be staring at the outline of her breasts beneath her blouse. Why couldn't adults just go about their business and leave sex for wedding nights and other appropriate occasions?

Putting on her contact lenses proved even more of a challenge because there was no stopper in the sink. Finally Kate laid a washcloth over the drain, just in case she dropped one.

When she emerged, Mitch handed her a plate but kept his gaze averted. Honestly! Anyone would think she was Medusa, whose image would turn him to stone.

They ate outside, to the delight of a pair of squirrels that kept darting in to grab crumbs. One of them flashed by so close its tail brushed Kate's ankle.

"They certainly are tame," she said.

"Wild animals should never get this used to people." Mitch finished another bite of waffle. "Somebody's likely to eat them for dinner."

"Are you always this cynical?" she asked.

"When a man lives close to nature, he has to take a realistic view." Lounging sideways on the picnic bench with his Stetson slightly askew, Mitch looked as if he were taking a break in the middle of a cattle drive.

Kate wondered what impression he made on clients. Maybe residents of Gulch City, Texas, were accustomed to cowboy lawyers.

After cleaning up, they headed for the freeway. Barely had they reached it when the truck began rattling and vibrating.

"What's wrong?" Kate glanced nervously at a highway patrol car cruising past.

Mitch grimaced. "Could be a lot of things. Lucky

we're near Fresno. On the other hand, it's Sunday. Not the best day to find spare parts.''

He wasn't kidding. The vibrations had worsened by the time they exited the freeway, and the morning droned by as he phoned all over town, then chugged the truck by fits and starts to the only secondhand parts yard that was open.

Kate sat on a rickety folding chair and watched while he made repairs. Every time a police car rolled by on the street, her throat tightened and her hands got clammy. Even though she'd done nothing wrong, she felt like a criminal.

Maybe she *had* done something wrong by not turning Mitch in. It was all very well to tell herself that she had him in custody, but she doubted a judge would see it that way. Especially since she wasn't even officially the sheriff yet.

Besides, she had no intention of locking him up. Maybe Mitch was guilty and lying like a rug, but Kate didn't think so. She'd always trusted her instincts, and they'd never led her wrong before.

The one good thing, she told herself, was that evidently Moose had respected her wishes and not called the authorities. He wasn't such a bad fellow, really.

He could be a lot of laughs, emceeing concerts in the park. They had fun at the high school football games, too, cheering alongside their friends.

Life with him wouldn't be bad. It would certainly beat sitting next to a broken-down truck watching Mitch, hands and face smeared with grease, poke through a pile of salvaged parts trying to find the one that fit.

She tried not to think about how that grease emphasized Mitch's high cheekbones, or how his eyes burned at her whenever he turned in her direction. When he took off his shirt and the sunlight gleamed on the golden expanse of his chest, she beat a hasty retreat behind one of her education journals.

By the time the truck purred once more, they were both exhausted. With little discussion, they returned to the same campsite for a second night.

At dinner, Kate found the squirrels more pesky than cute. But at least, the next morning, Mitch hightailed it out of the camper in a hurry when she was ready to get dressed.

AT THE SUNGOLD HILLS Academy of Music, glass buildings reflected the rolling emerald lawns and lavender-plumed jacaranda trees. It looked a lot more modern than the law school Mitch had attended.

"You suppose this Horst fellow is still around?" he asked as they strode along the sidewalk. "Loretta graduated last year."

"I got the impression he was a few years younger than Loretta," Kate answered.

Just before they arrived, she had changed into her tailored jacket and slacks. Mitch had figured at first it was female vanity, but now he could see that her professional image made them look more like visiting professors than intruders.

Loretta must have enjoyed this place, Mitch mused as they passed a flower bed spilling over with fanciful yellow-and-orange poppies. He wondered, though, if it had seemed kind of tame, given the way she liked to hop onto a quarter horse and head out onto the range to round up stray calves.

It had been a shock when she turned up four months ago to take a job as secretary of the building-supply business that Billy had started at the ranch. Mitch almost didn't recognize her the first time he saw her in town, buying computer paper at the general store.

The chubby teenaged figure had slimmed down and the wiry brown hair had been tamed into collar-length waves. When she spotted him, her olive-colored eyes narrowed, and she'd turned away.

He'd tried to talk with her several times, even calling her at the ranch. Finally she'd E-mailed him to say that she had no interest in speaking with him, then or ever.

People in Gulch City had speculated that Billy might have made some kind of deal with her, maybe to prevent her from joining Mitch's lawsuit. Grandpa hadn't left a written will, but since Loretta's parents never showed any interest in running the ranch, it had come to Mitch's father by default.

Loretta might have a legal claim to share in the ownership. But even if she was willing to sell her half to Billy, that didn't explain why she would choose to work for him.

Or why she had run out on Mitch when her testimony was the only thing standing between him and a possible death sentence. Could she really be that angry, or was she afraid for her own safety?

He wanted some answers, and with Kate's help he might get them today.

They went up a set of wide steps into the administration building. Kate asked the way to the registrar's office in such authoritative tones that the cheeky-looking receptionist called her ma'am when she answered.

The building's soaring interior echoed with the click of Mitch's boots as they followed the young woman's directions. There was hardly anyone around, he noted as they circled an indoor fountain beneath a glass dome. Why had the college built itself such a palace?

He supposed that modern-day administrators must have the same mind-set as pharaohs in ancient Egypt. They built huge edifices, not because they needed them, but because being surrounded by grandeur made their own puny selves seem more magnificent.

It was not a charitable observation. But in his quest for legal justice, Mitch had received shoddy treatment from bureaucrats and magistrates in architecturally pretentious halls back in Texas, and he still held a grudge.

At the registrar's office, they were confronted by a broad marble counter large enough to accommodate a dozen clerks. The entire outer room was staffed by a single woman, so young she might even be a student.

Again, Kate's confident manner worked its magic. The clerk couldn't reveal Horst's off-campus address or telephone number, but she confirmed that he was still enrolled.

"He's probably signed up for one of the practice rooms." She gave them a campus map and circled Building E. "You'll find the students' names posted on schedules on the doors. Or you could stick a note on the bulletin board in the cafeteria."

"We'll try the practice rooms," Kate said. "Thank you." They exited the cool building into the warm day and followed the map.

As they approached Building E, Mitch heard the faint rumble of pianos and staccato bursts of song. Apparently even soundproofing didn't completely contain the noise.

Melodies and rhythms collided in the spring air. Not

only was the sound jarring, but, given the way people kept starting and stopping, Mitch wondered how they ever worked up to an entire performance.

At the ranch, his grandmother had sung effortlessly, although in a voice thinned by age. As a youngster, Loretta had mimicked her with ease.

Since then, he knew that she'd soloed with her church choir and won several voice competitions. Mitch had never given much thought to what she might have studied at music school, though. He'd assumed that, when she sang, she simply opened her mouth and let the lovely sounds fly out.

Now, hearing an older woman command a student to watch her phrasing, it occurred to him that the world of serious music was as alien to him as rocket science. He didn't even know what *phrasing* meant.

At the moment, it didn't matter. The finer points of culture had vanished from Mitch's sphere of attention ten years ago. And presumably from Loretta's when she decided to get mixed up with the ranch.

Ahead of him, Kate tapped up the steps into the building. They entered a hallway lined by heavy doors, each with a small window and, below it, a sheet with times and names.

According to a posted notice, students could sign up to use the practice rooms for one hour at a time. Anyone who was more than five minutes late risked losing the room to the first comer.

"Let's split up," Kate said. "You check that side."

"Right." Mitch began skimming the lists.

He had made it halfway down the corridor when a bell clanged, so loud he flinched. Kate hardly seemed to notice, at least not until the rehearsal rooms banged open and students stampeded out.

''Must be lunchtime!'' Mitch called above the thundering herd.

She made a face, but didn't try to shout over the din. From her frown, however, he got the impression that youngsters at Kate's school would never, ever dare behave in such an uncouth manner.

Then Kate turned abruptly as, swimming against the tide, a young man shouldered his way toward one of the rooms. He had a slight build and a thin face with a beaked nose. His most prominent feature, however, was a thick mop of shaggy black hair.

''Horst!'' Kate called.

The fellow stopped elbowing through the crowd just long enough to be swept back toward the exit. With a fierce shake, he pushed himself free and stood his ground until the hall cleared. Kate began to introduce herself, but he interrupted, recognizing her.

''Are you looking for Loretta, too?''

''What do you mean, *too?*'' Mitch demanded.

The young man regarded him dubiously. ''Who are you?''

''Horst, this is Loretta's cousin Mitch.'' Kate strode forward. She was only an inch or two shorter than the young man.

''The one who threw away the High C?'' Horst asked.

Mitch sighed. He was gladder than ever that he'd brought Kate along to explain things. And to keep him from strangling this young fool.

''It was stolen, and I'm trying to get it back,'' he said. ''Who else was looking for my cousin? She could be in danger.''

''Danger?'' Although the crowd had gone, Horst remained planted in the center of the hallway. ''From those men? They said she left something valuable at the ranch and their boss had sent them to return it. You mean they might have been lying?'' He sounded shocked.

"When did they come by?" Kate asked.

"Early this morning." Horst shifted his backpack, which hung heavily from his slim shoulders. "Maybe nine o'clock. They woke me up."

"At nine?" Mitch couldn't resist a touch of irony. A cowboy's day began before sunup. Lazing about until seven was reserved for the occasional Sunday, and then only if there were no calves being born and no bad weather on the horizon.

The student drew himself up as best he could, given his weighty backpack. "I have to conserve my voice. Early mornings are murder."

The last word hung in the air. Horst didn't seem to notice, which meant Loretta at least hadn't described Mitch as a killer.

Other students began filtering in, heading for the practice rooms. Horst glanced reluctantly at one of the lists, then said, "Well, I guess this is going to take a while. I'll come back later and hope somebody else misses their turn."

"Have you eaten?" Kate asked. When he shook his head, she said, "I'll treat."

The young man perked up immediately. In fact, as they clattered down the steps together, his jaw loosened noticeably.

"We're talking about three guys, cowboy types?" he said. "Kind of an odd trio, like something from a comic opera? They must have found my address among Loretta's stuff. I guess she left the ranch in a hurry."

"You guess?" said Kate. "You haven't seen her?"

"Uh, yeah, she showed up last week." Horst scurried toward the student union so fast Mitch had to take longer strides, and Kate was nearly trotting. "She seemed really rattled. She told me she drove straight through from Texas, but she wouldn't say why."

Mitch was relieved to realize he'd been correct about Loretta going to California. "How long ago did she leave?"

"Let's see." Horst's cheeks twitched. "Okay, she got here on Thursday and made a few phone calls, like she was real agitated, and then—"

"Hi, Howie!" called a striking African-American woman. "Loved your aria at the concert Friday!"

"'*Di Quella Pira?*'" he asked hopefully.

"Oh, I didn't mean that one," she admitted. "I'm not sure you're quite ready for Verdi. '*Una Furtiva Lagrima,*' that was terrific. I love Donizetti and besides, light opera is more your thing, don't you think?"

He smiled, but not very enthusiastically. The woman turned to greet some other people, and Mitch felt a spurt of sympathy for Horst, whose ambitions apparently exceeded his capabilities.

"Why did she call you Howie?" Kate asked. "I thought your name was Horst."

They took a side entrance into the student union. "Well, yeah," said their guide. "I mean, it's Howard Wells, but who wants to go hear a singer with a name like that? Look at the big stars—Placido Domingo, Kiri Te Kanawa, Bryn Terfel. Isn't that a great name, Bryn Terfel? I wish I were Welsh."

"Horst Wittgenstein sounds German," Kate noted. They entered a huge dining hall, a sea of noise and motion, and Mitch surveyed it uneasily for anyone or anything out of place. Especially cops, or bandits with shotguns.

There weren't any. At least, not that he could see.

Horst led them into the cafeteria line. "I figured I could pass for at least part-German."

He piled his tray high with a salad, side dishes, two entrées, dessert and juice. "Somebody else must be paying," remarked a heavyset young man as he walked by.

"Don't mind him," said Horst. "Baritones are always jealous of tenors."

To Mitch, the pasta looked overcooked. He selected a corned beef sandwich on rye instead. Kate picked a chef's salad.

They found an empty table in a corner. "When did Loretta leave?" Kate asked.

"Yesterday." Horst dug into his food and came up chewing. "A friend of hers arranged for an audition in Santa Fe. There's a new low-budget opera company starting up to take advantage of the crowds they get in the summer. They're doing *Così Fan Tutte*."

Mitch couldn't believe it. "You mean the only thing on Loretta's mind was getting a part in a show?"

Horst stiffened. "Mozart did not write *shows*."

"We need to find her," Kate said. "We don't believe those men want to return something to Loretta. We think they want to make sure she doesn't testify against them in a murder case."

Horst's jaw dropped open. Thank goodness, it was momentarily empty of food. "Really? Gosh, she never mentioned that. But there *was* something she was trying to find at the ranch, so I figured that was what they wanted to return."

Loretta had been searching for something? The discovery was, for Mitch, like getting an unexpected peek through a curtain.

His cousin's decision to work for Billy Parkinson made at least a little sense if her intent had been to retrieve something from the High C. He leaned forward. "What exactly was it?"

"I don't know." Horst resumed eating. "All I told those three guys was, 'Well, gee, she'll be glad you found it.' The young one got kind of threatening and demanded to know how much I knew about 'it' and I admitted I didn't have any precise information, so to speak."

Mitch groaned inwardly. Now that Horst had opened his big mouth, Billy would have even more reason to track down his cousin.

But then, the man had probably gone on the alert the minute Loretta turned up at the ranch to apply for a job. Mitch had wondered at the time why Billy would hire her, when Loretta might presumably be an enemy.

The girl was so naive, it wouldn't have occurred to her that Billy would assume she had some ulterior motive. He'd probably been watching her the whole time.

The ranch's basement storage rooms were filled with furniture and memorabilia. He supposed valuables could have been hidden somewhere, perhaps in a secret compartment or drawer. Billy must have hoped Loretta would sniff them out.

Kate was speaking again. "We need to warn her that this gang is coming. Is there some way to contact her?"

"Well, she left her friend's P.O. box for forwarding mail."

"Did you give it to the three men?" Mitch asked.

Horst nodded guiltily. "I figured, if they only wanted to return something, maybe they could mail it." His voice trailed off.

"If they were willing to mail it, they wouldn't have driven to California."

The young man flinched. "Yeah, I guess not."

Kate didn't waste time on reproaches. "Do you know anything that could help us find her before they do?"

"They didn't ask who she was auditioning for," Horst offered. "It's called the Pocket Opera Company. They might be listed with information."

"What about her friend, the one who set it up?" Mitch demanded. "Maybe we can contact her."

Horst shrugged. "Her first name is Sally. That's all I know."

"If you hear from Loretta, tell her to get out of Santa Fe," Kate said. "Those guys are armed."

His thin face paled, which made the mop of dark hair stand out even more. "Maybe we ought to call the police."

Just what they needed, Mitch thought. The way his luck was running, he'd get to Santa Fe to find the cops waiting for him.

Kate frowned. "You can call them if you like, but I doubt they'll stake out a post office box based on such sketchy information."

"But if these guys are wanted for murder..."

"They aren't," she said. "I'm the sheriff in Grazer's Corners, and I'm seeking them for shooting up the town. Mitch has reason to believe they're connected to an even more serious crime in Texas, but no charges have been filed."

"Gosh, this is weird." Horst moved on to dessert, a large slab of chocolate cake. "I never thought I'd get involved in anything like this. And I sure wouldn't want anyone to hurt Loretta. She has a great voice. I mean, she could really be somebody."

"She's somebody now," Mitch growled. "She would be, whether she could sing or not."

The youthful bluster vanished as Horst set down his fork and met Mitch's gaze. "I know that, but she doesn't. She's never really believed in herself. She wouldn't have dared to go to the ranch if it weren't for something you said, Ms. Bingham."

"Me?" Kate's voice had a hoarse edge.

"At the scholarship lunch," Horst said. "You talked about never giving up, about taking risks for what you really believe in. About sorting out your priorities and then living by them."

"I guess I did say that," she conceded.

"It rang a bell with Loretta," Horst continued. "After that, she kind of changed. She said she owed it to her grandmother to set things right. After a while, it became like an obsession."

"Whatever she was seeking, you don't have a clue what it is?" Mitch pressed.

"She never said." Horst's attention returned to the chocolate cake.

It seemed they had exhausted the sum total of the young man's knowledge, at least as far as Loretta was concerned. They obtained the post office box number, along with Horst's promise to mail an overnight letter to Loretta that afternoon, warning her about the bandits.

But Mitch couldn't rely on her receiving it in time. This Sally might not pick up her mail every day, and she might not deliver the letter immediately even if she did.

As they said goodbye to Horst, he tried to reassure himself that, given Kate's way with receptionists and officials, they could locate his cousin in Santa Fe before Tiny Wheeler did. Then he remembered that Kate was planning to take a bus directly back to Grazer's Corners, and Moose.

He couldn't fault the lady for being loyal to her fiancé. Besides, the rescue of his cousin was Mitch's job, and no one else's.

They wended their way through swirls of students and out to the walkway. Mitch matched his pace to Kate's moderate one, torn between an instinct to hurry and a reluctance to say farewell to her.

"This thing that Loretta's looking for," Kate said. "Could it be money?"

"No. She wouldn't risk her life for that. It must have some kind of sentimental value. Maybe financial as well, though."

"Like jewelry?"

Mitch pictured the stored clutter of furniture, boxes and chests. He wasn't sure exactly what they contained, although he recalled seeing some photographs and gowns. Personal papers, sheet music and a few books, too. Nothing with any obvious value.

"Grandma Luisa might have owned some jewelry, but I'd be surprised if she didn't give it all to her daughter. The antiques could be worth something, and perhaps the collection of costumes, but I don't see how Loretta could have planned to sneak them out."

"Whatever she's looking for, it must be small." They reached the parking lot. "A rare musical instrument? A violin, maybe?"

"If so, I never saw it," Mitch said. "We had an excellent piano, but she could hardly have slipped that off the premises without being seen."

Kate fidgeted while he unlocked the pickup. "Surely Billy would have searched through everything by now. How could he miss it?"

Mitch held the door for her. "There's a lot of stuff. And he wouldn't know what he was looking for. Grandma had some programs signed by famous singers and conductors. They might be worth something to a collector."

He came around to the driver's side. As soon as he got in, Kate said, "I can't help thinking it must be something even more personal. Maybe a diary…"

Mitch switched on the motor. "Any idea where the bus station is?"

"The bus station?"

"That's where you wanted to go, isn't it?"

Startled blue eyes blinked at him. "I can't quit now. Loretta took these crazy risks because of me."

"My cousin is twenty-five years old and she's responsible for her own life," Mitch said. "Of course, I intend to do everything in my power to help her. But it's not your fault if she seized on some remark you made."

"Yes, it is." Kate's jaw tightened. "As a person who spends her life working with young people, it's my duty to consider how my comments may affect them."

"You couldn't have known that she'd go tearing off to Texas and sign on with a crooked rancher!"

"Intentionally or not, I set this mess into motion," she said. "I couldn't live with myself if I abandoned Loretta now."

It took Mitch about thirty seconds to realize that he didn't want to argue any further. "Okay by me."

"We can take turns sleeping outside," she offered.

The heck they would. "We'll discuss it later."

"Got a map? We'll need to figure out the shortest route to Santa Fe."

"I already know. I just drove here, remember? I didn't go through Santa Fe, but I went near it." Another thought occurred to Mitch, one he'd considered on the way west but hadn't had time to indulge. "We have to cut through Flagstaff. The doctor who loaned the money to my Dad used to own a cabin south of there, in Oak Creek Canyon. It's possible his daughter might have returned by now. There's no phone on the premises, but we could swing by."

"As long as we don't get sidetracked for long."

"Don't worry," he said. "I want to protect Loretta as much as you do."

Kate settled back. They were approaching the 210 Freeway, which would take them east on the first leg of their journey, when she sat bolt upright.

"Oh, my gosh!" she said. "This means I'll be gone a lot longer than I expected. A whole lot longer! I have to call Moose...but what am I going to tell him?"

Chapter Six

For a moment, Kate wished that Mitch had a car phone. Then she realized that, if he did, she would have to give Moose the number, and she found herself reluctant to be at his beck and call.

Still, she drummed her fingers impatiently on the armrest as they traveled, keeping watch for a freeway exit where they might find a telephone. She didn't know what she was going to say, but she wanted to get this over with.

He might not understand. Moose shared some of her values, but not all of them.

And, she had to admit, she was putting him in an awkward position. Not only had his wedding been disrupted, but his bride had gone on the lam with a criminal. Suspected criminal, she amended hastily.

Until now, choices had been simple in Kate's life. There was right, and there was wrong. The difference had always been obvious.

But now the issues were getting muddied. She owed a duty to Moose, and also to Loretta. Since the young woman was more vulnerable, and in a sense had been endangered because of Kate, she seemed to have the more immediate claim.

Am I being completely honest with myself? Tearing her gaze from the roadside tracts of houses, Kate turned to study Mitch.

Despite his attention to the traffic, there was a far-away look in his eyes. Perhaps he was seeing the ranch that he still called home. Or maybe he was working through scenarios of what might lie ahead.

What was it about him that fascinated her? Why did she get goose bumps just looking at him?

It must be an intellectual challenge, she told herself. Never in her well-ordered life had she met anyone like Mitch.

She came from a place where everybody knew everybody else's business; he lived, at least for the present, outside society. In her world, the only challenges were personal or financial. In his world, the stakes were life and death.

But why did she want so strongly to help clear his name? The fact that he'd saved her life might partly explain it. So might anger at the gang that had invaded her life and her town. But that couldn't be the whole story.

The shocking realization hit Kate that she wasn't ready to get married. She'd never been aware of a yearning for adventure, for pushing limits and striking out into the unknown, yet here it was, and here was the man who had inspired it.

She wondered what her parents would have said. She supposed they might have told her that it couldn't hurt to spend a little time away from Moose and Grazer's Corners, until she felt more at peace.

Absence made the heart grow fonder, didn't it? By the time she got home, surely all her hesitations would vanish. Once she stretched her legs a bit, she would be ready to settle down with Moose, and that silly image of his house barred like a prison would never recur.

It seemed like fate that, at the precise moment that she resolved her uncertainties, she spotted a gas station. It was a shiny new building, and would almost certainly have a working phone.

MOOSE STOOD IN FRONT of Harmon's Department Store, inhaling the balmy air. He could smell hamburger grease from Good Eats, and a hint of manure from the farmlands outside town. Come to think of it, it was hard to tell which scent was which.

Behind him, he felt Betty Muller's woebegone stare through the glass doors. She'd been moping around the cosmetics counter all morning.

Well, he knew she was downhearted, but it couldn't be helped. Betty would have to resign herself to losing at love.

On Almond Grove Avenue, just past the offices of the *Grazer Gazette*, Agatha Flintstone emerged from the Book Nook. Since she owned the place, she often went in during her lunch hour to check on the clerk and sort through the latest romance novels.

Romance novels! Moose thought with a mental snort. He was glad his Kate wasn't the sort of addle-pated female who expected a knight in shining armor to sweep her away.

Across the square, Jeanie Jeffrey trotted out of town hall carrying a cordless phone. "Yoo-hoo!" she yelled. "Mr. Harmon! I need you!"

Moose's chest swelled. He'd gone from being Big Man on Campus at Grazer State to Big Man in Town, and it felt good.

He set out down the block at a trot, picturing a football tucked under one arm and a herd of bruisers heading in his direction. Instinctively, Moose put his head down to cut the drag, and barely looked up in time to avoid smacking into Agatha.

"Well!" She took a quick step backward, clutching her pile of paperbacks.

"My apologies, Miss Flintstone." He felt like a schoolboy caught smoking in the rest room. "I was just—"

"Moose! I really need you to take this call!" Jeanie shouted from the opposite corner.

"Okay, coming." He hurried to her and snatched the receiver. "This is Bledsoe Harmon, mayor of Grazer's Corners. To whom am I speaking?"

The response was a burst of static, then silence.

"You took the phone out of range!" he accused Jeanie.

Her square face crumpled. "I'm sorry, Mr. Harmon. It was the police chief from Gulch City, Texas, and I didn't know what to tell him."

Grumbling, Moose followed her through the town hall courtyard to the sheriff's office. "I suppose he'll call back."

"Oh, and I needed to ask you something." Jeanie picked a string off her dress and tossed it onto the floor. "See, I was supposed to take my vacation next week. I made the reservations and bought my tickets to Hawaii already. I know Kate will be back, but then you'll go on your honeymoon, and without Sheriff Brockner..."

"Don't you worry," Moose said. "You go ahead and take your vacation. I'll make sure somebody covers for you."

"Thanks!" She beamed at him as she dialed the phone. "I'll try long distance information—maybe we can get a number for the Gulch City police."

He was about to point out that if she tied up the line, the chief couldn't reach them, but just then his cell phone rang.

Moose whipped it from the pocket inside his jacket. "Yes?"

"It's me." That was Kate. "Moose, I'm going to be gone a little longer than I thought."

His neck started getting hot. "Why is that?"

"You remember Loretta Blaine, who sings at church?" He nodded, then remembered that she couldn't see him. "Well, she's Mitch's cousin and she's in a lot of danger, and it's because of my advice. So we have to go to Santa Fe."

"Santa Fe?" he roared.

"We'll stop in some place south of Flagstaff, I think it's called Oak Creek Canyon, to see someone who might be able to help Mitch—see, his ranch was stolen—and then we need to reach Loretta before they do."

"Who are 'they'?"

"Those men who shot up the church," she said. "The Tiny Wheeler Gang."

He couldn't believe this. Sure, he'd seen those bandits, and there were bullet holes in the church walls to prove the guns had been real, but the name Tiny Wheeler Gang sounded as if it came from a Wild West movie. "What kind of rubbish is this?"

"I know it sounds strange," Kate continued in her maddeningly level voice. "But I couldn't be the woman you love if I didn't fulfill my duty."

"Your duty is to me!"

"And I intend to fulfill that, too," she said, as if she were referring to a speaking engagement instead of a marriage. "We can't get the church again on a Saturday for two or three weeks anyway, and I absolutely promise I'll be back by then."

"Three weeks?" He nearly strangled over all those long-*E* sounds. "Kate!"

"Just think what a great story this will make to tell our children!" she said cheerily. "Bye, Moose." And hung up.

He wanted to yank the phone out of the wall, but he couldn't. That was the darned problem with cell phones.

Jeanie, on her line, scribbled down a number and hung up. It rang again immediately.

"Hello?" she said. "Oh, hi, Chief. I've been trying to get your number, that's why it was busy.... There's no need to shout.... I'll just let you talk to the mayor now, sir." She rubbed her ear and handed Moose the receiver.

"Mayor Harmon here!" he snapped.

"This is Chief Norris Novo in Gulch City, Texas." The man's softly accented voice carried an edge of irritation. "I am trying to track down a lead from one of our citizens, a Mr. Billy Parkinson, who says a wanted murderer may have been seen in your town."

"Are you referring to Mitch Connery?"

"You've seen him?" said Chief Novo.

"Yes, sir, I have." Finding himself a key witness soothed Moose's ruffled feathers slightly. "He disrupted a church service and took off with..." How could he admit that his bride had been stolen? And if he said the sheriff had been snatched, it would make the whole town look like Podunk Station. "...with our elementary school principal. I believe he conned her with some story about being framed.''

''I wouldn't put it past him. He's a smooth talker,'' said the chief. ''Got any idea where they're headed?''

''As a matter of fact, I do.'' Moose relayed the information about Flagstaff and Santa Fe.

''Thank you very kindly,'' said Chief Novo. ''By the way, how come I'm talking to the mayor? Don't you have some kind of law out there?''

''In Grazer's Corners?'' retorted Moose. ''Nothing ever happens here.''

''Other than shoot-outs in church?'' drawled the chief. ''In any case, I do appreciate your help.''

''You're welcome.'' Moose handed the receiver to Jeanie.

Then he realized he'd forgotten to mention that the Tiny Wheeler Gang was hot on Mitch's tail. But he supposed Chief Novo already knew that.

''You did a great job! Thanks for taking the call,'' Jeanie said. ''Grazer's Corners would be lost without you, Mr. Harmon.''

He smiled in gracious acknowledgment. Then his expansive mood evaporated as he remembered that Kate wasn't coming back for a while.

Doggone it, what was a man supposed to do, eat frozen dinners and watch reruns on TV when he should be enjoying his honeymoon? It would serve her right if he did ask Betsy out to dinner.

In fact, he thought as he went out the door, he was going to do exactly that.

THE SAN BERNARDINO MOUNTAINS were noted for their scenic vistas and for the ski resorts of Lake Arrowhead and Big Bear. In Kate's memory, however, they would always be associated with long steep grades on which the pickup whined and groaned like a mammoth on the verge of extinction.

Was this, she wondered, where the Donner Party had gotten stuck during pioneer days and spent a terrible winter, eventually sinking to cannibalism? No, she remembered with a twinge of relief, that was further north in the Sierra Nevada.

"Is something making you nervous?" asked Mitch.

Kate glanced at her hands and saw that her nails had cut half-moons into her palms. "I guess I don't like heights."

"Going up or coming down?" he asked.

That brought up another, even more frightening thought. "How good are your brakes?"

"Well, they made it west okay," he said. "Frankly, I never gave it much thought. The landscape's pretty flat around Gulch City and this old beast's been real reliable for hauling calves."

"You haul a lot of calves in the lawyer business?" She tried to ignore a zillion-foot drop into forested depths, just inches from the road's shoulder.

"Not for the past ten years," Mitch conceded. "I never bothered to buy a car because I always figured I'd be getting the High C back. Besides, I couldn't afford to."

"The camper looks...almost new." She winced as a car with peeling paint and a souped-up engine screeched uphill past them.

"I got it cheap because the inside was trashed." Mitch rested one forearm atop the wheel. "I made the cabinets myself."

That *did* impress Kate. "Where'd you learn to do that?"

"A cowboy needs woodworking skills," he explained. "You've got to be able to fend for yourself if you get cut off from town. Throw up a fence, fix the roof, whatever."

"Do you really get cut off?" The image she formed was not an unpleasant one, of a picture-postcard farmhouse with lights glowing against the snow. On the other hand, in these days when you could contact someone on the other side of the globe in seconds via the Internet, isolation seemed like a relic from another century.

"Oh, we can get a helicopter to fly in if there's a medical emergency," he admitted. "But that's not much help if a horse kicks a hole in your corral. Plus we get twisters now and then. You can't be calling out a carpenter all the time." His tone implied that a real man would always exhaust his own resources before summoning help.

"You're not going to turn macho on me, are you?"

He regarded her in surprise. "What do you mean by that?"

"Toughing everything out by yourself." Kate wriggled in the seat, wishing she'd changed back to jeans and jogging shoes before they left Pasadena. "I figured you were an equal opportunity cowboy."

Mitch's gaze swung back to the highway. "Taking care of your own business isn't what I call macho. That's just the way people do things when they live close to nature."

"What would you call macho?"

"Throwing your weight around," he said promptly. "Strutting like a peacock, getting jealous for no reason, starting a fight because some fellow looks at you cross-eyed."

"I guess you're right," Kate admitted. She'd simply assumed that masculine independence and self-sufficiency were signs of machismo.

Specializing in the education field, she was accustomed to teamwork and committees and deferring to accepted authorities. But a man or woman who lived on a ranch would need a different mind-set, tougher and more individualistic.

Those were qualities she was coming to appreciate more and more since she'd met Mitch. He didn't see any need to show off; he just quietly went about getting things done, even when those things involved danger.

Unlike Moose, he would certainly never cower in safety while his fiancée was abducted from their wedding. Not that she'd been abducted, exactly. And Moose, she reminded herself, hadn't cowered. He'd fled with the minister in tow.

They were in the Victorville area, past the turnoff to the Roy Rogers-Dale Evans Museum, when the truck heaved a long sigh that developed into a steamy hiss. They barely managed to limp along to the next gas station.

How would they ever make it Flagstaff, let alone Santa Fe, if the truck kept breaking down?

"Probably needs a new thermostat," Mitch advised as he pulled alongside the station's repair bay. "Might take an hour or so."

Kate peered unhappily at the sky. The sun was sinking and darkness moving in fast. Clouds formed a high canopy.

The last weather report on the radio hadn't mentioned rain. She took some comfort in that, at least.

By the time Mitch diagnosed the problem, bought

the proper part and fixed the truck, darkness had descended. The first campground they saw had a No Vacancy sign, and the second was little more than a parking lot. There was no place for Mitch to sleep outdoors.

Kate didn't want to press on in the dark, not in view of the steepness of the terrain and the fragility of the truck. Neither did she want to find herself crammed into close quarters with Mitch.

"We could go on," he said. "Or we could make the best of things and share the camper."

A few years back, Kate and Moose had gone fishing with friends and ended up sharing a tent. A small tent, at that. After a few hopeful glances and a sloppy kiss, Moose had left her alone, and she'd slept like a baby.

She didn't think she would sleep like a baby in the same room with Mitch. And she didn't want to go down the mountain in the dark.

"Drop me at a motel," she said.

"You sure?" There was no criticism in his tone, only concern. "You use a credit card, somebody could trace you."

"I'm not wanted for anything," she said. "And I don't think Moose is going to fire up his Lincoln and come charging after me."

"I would," Mitch said quietly. "If you belonged to me."

The words sent a quiver up Kate's spine. Rather than try to figure out what it meant, she teased, "You mean you'd rope me and lasso me and carry me home?"

"I'd make sure you were all right." The truck turned onto the highway. "And if you needed my help, I'd come with you."

"Even to clear another man's name?"

"If you believed in him, I'd give it serious consideration." They drove for another mile or so, then pulled into a motel lot. "This place look okay?"

"Just fine," Kate said.

"I'll pick you up at seven-thirty." He indicated the motel's restaurant. "That way you can enjoy a civilized breakfast."

"Thanks."

After retrieving her suitcase, Kate watched the truck pull away with an unfamiliar sense of loss. She hardly knew the man, yet she missed him already.

She checked in, walked up a flight of stairs and let herself into Number 25. Plopping her suitcase on the bed, Kate stared around the motel room as if she had just arrived in a foreign country. After the busy last few days, it felt peculiar to find herself alone.

Well, it wasn't as if she'd never traveled before. She attended education-related conferences several times a year, and basically all hotel chambers looked alike. She pulled a few items from her suitcase and went to take a long, hot shower.

After she dried off, she noticed there was a telephone in the room. She could call Moose and have a private chat. But she didn't want to.

To her surprise, Kate didn't miss Grazer's Corners. She didn't wish she was having a night of wedded bliss with Moose and she didn't miss the books that usually surrounded her at home.

In fact, when she thought of home, she kept picturing the warm cedar-scented interior of the camper, with Mitch cooking pasta at the stove. That must be the problem: she was hungry.

Retrieving an education journal to read while she ate, Kate dressed and went to the restaurant.

THE SKY HAD TURNED a relentless slate gray by morning. Suitcase packed and bill paid, Kate finished a leisurely breakfast by the coffee shop window where she could watch for Mitch.

Outside, a highway patrol car pulled in. Kate's heart thudded into her throat.

The cruiser slotted itself between a motor home and a minivan. At this angle, she doubted Mitch would see it when he arrived.

Kate checked her watch. It was 7:28. She hoped Mitch would be late.

It was even possible that he wouldn't come at all. Last night, she'd given him the perfect opportunity to go his own way unfettered.

A yearning tightened her chest. She didn't want the adventure to end yet. Besides, for all his resourcefulness, Mitch needed her help.

The door jingled open and the highway patrolman entered the nearly empty restaurant. He was of average height and slightly stocky.

"Coffee?" asked the hostess.

"Sure." He followed her past Kate to the next booth. As he went by, he gave her a pleasant nod, which she returned.

There was still no sign of the truck. Kate hoped the patrolman would drink quickly and leave.

Her hopes faded as the waitress sauntered to his booth and, after setting down the coffee, flipped open her pad. "What'll it be? The usual?"

Kate couldn't see the man, but she could hear his

deep sigh. "No, thanks. I'll take some cereal. That high-fiber stuff. The kind with no taste."

A low rumble from outside startled Kate. But it was just a kid on a skateboard, hitting every crack and bump in the pavement with bone-crunching determination.

"You can't give up on doughnuts *today!*" teased the waitress. "We've got some fresh made."

"I'm trying to cut down." After a moment, the patrolman said, "Got any jelly?"

"Sure." Even without looking, Kate could hear the smile in the waitress's voice.

The patrolman groaned. "Give me two, will you?"

"Two?"

"Make that three."

"You got it." The woman moved away.

The man was sitting behind Kate, hidden by the booth divider. But whatever she could view out the window, so could he.

So he probably saw, as soon as she did, the battered pickup with a camper on the back as it turned into the lot. Texas plates. And the number, she remembered, was listed on the APB.

Mitch rolled past the restaurant. Kate waved through the window, and saw his answering signal.

She tried to gesture him to go on and park, but he stopped directly in front of them. The patrolman couldn't help seeing him.

Fighting down a wave of panic, she picked up the check, grabbed her suitcase and moved to the cash register. *Mitch, move the truck. Drive on past and you'll see the patrol car.*

Maybe he would realize the danger and just keep

going on to Flagstaff without her. It would be better than getting caught.

As she stood at the counter, fishing her wallet from her purse, she listened for the patrolman to call in a report. Surely he had a portable phone or radio with him.

The hostess appeared and took Kate's money. It was such a relief, her knees wobbled. Now all she had to do was walk slowly out of here and they'd be safe....

Then she remembered that she hadn't put down a tip. She couldn't walk away and leave the waitress empty-handed.

Kate dug for a dollar. She only had a twenty. "Could you break this? I forgot the tip."

The hostess began counting change, then stopped as the phone rang. "Motel restaurant. Sure, we're easy to find. Take the Palmdale Road exit..."

Kate couldn't believe it. Mitch was going to get sent to the electric chair because she didn't have a buck for a tip.

"No, we're on the right..." Whoever was calling must have had difficulty hearing, because the hostess had to repeat everything several times.

Agonizing moments later, she hung up and finished her task. Kate handed back a dollar. "Give this to the waitress, will you?"

"Sure thing."

She stepped back and bumped into someone. Someone tall and solid, but not as tall and solid as Mitch.

"Sorry." Kate glanced up, directly into the expressionless eyes of the highway patrolman. Her whole body went cold, and she could barely force out the word, "Yes?"

"That your friend out there in the truck?"

She couldn't deny it; he must have seen Mitch wave. "Yes, sir."

"Well, he forgot to latch the door in the back of the camper. I noticed it when he pulled in."

Kate resisted the urge to sag against the counter. "Thank you. I'll tell him."

"Wouldn't want you folks losing your possessions all over the interstate." The patrolman shook his head. "Inconvenient for you, and a heck of a mess to clean up."

She gave him a weak smile and went out. Mitch came around the front of the cab to open her door.

With her back to the coffee shop, Kate said, "The camper door's open, and there's a highway patrolman about six feet from you inside the restaurant."

"I know." Mitch didn't blink an eye as he helped her in. "I didn't notice him until I was stopped, and then I decided it was better to act casual."

"Well, act casual quickly because I'm about to have a heart attack," she said, and gave him the suitcase.

The truck rocked as he stowed the case away, then closed and secured the camper door. The driver's door opened and he got in beside her. "He didn't suspect anything?"

Kate glanced into the café. A plate of doughnuts had the patrolman's full attention. "Nope."

"Nope?" Mitch started the motor and they pulled away. "You don't sound much like a school principal today."

"I don't feel like one. I feel like I'm starring in a low-budget remake of 'The Fugitive,'" she said.

"I've felt like that for the past ten days," Mitch agreed.

Her heartbeat slowed gradually from machine-gun

staccato to near-normal. As it did, Kate became aware of the wonderful scent filling the cab, cedar and spice and a hint of motor oil.

Despite the coolness of the day, it felt warm in here. That warmth, she knew without checking, didn't emanate from the truck's heater. In fact, given the general decrepitude of this vehicle, she doubted the heater even worked.

It came from Mitch. And it was as much psychological as physical.

AS THE DAY PASSED, the truck's steady rhythm made her doze. When she awoke, the landscape appeared unchanged, except for the addition of a few stark, crooked Joshua trees.

They were passing the East Mojave National Scenic Area when a faint pattering made Kate frown. For a moment she feared the truck was breaking down again, and then she saw raindrops speckling the bug-smeared windshield.

"I was hoping to make Kingman tonight, but I think we'd better find a place to pull over." Mitch's voice had a tight quality that inspired Kate to check her side-view mirror for some sign of pursuit. She didn't see any.

"You sound as if something's wrong," she said.

"You slept through the last weather report." He slowed to fifty-five miles per hour and turned on the headlights as the rain spatter thickened. "They're predicting heavy showers and a possibility of flash flooding."

"Surely not on the interstate," she returned.

"I wouldn't think so either, but the visibility's pretty low and it could drop to near zero." In the lane beside them, a semitrailer roared by as if they were standing still. ''Given the speed people drive around here, we're in danger of getting rear-ended.''

''I don't suppose your tires have a lot of tread to spare, either.'' A downpour heavy enough to create flash flooding might slicken the road and send them hydroplaning into oblivion. ''I've always wanting to try waterskiing, but not in a truck.''

''My tires are okay.'' Mitch peered ahead. ''Except for the left front one. I haven't been able to replace it because I don't dare use my credit cards.''

''That's reassuring.'' Kate took a deep breath. When she'd signed on for a bit of risk, she hadn't considered bald tires and desert floods, but it was too late to chicken out. Not that she wanted to. ''There!'' She pointed to an exit sign. ''We can get off here!''

''Yes, ma'am,'' Mitch said, and signaled a turn.

The rain intensified as they left the highway and eased down the ramp. There wasn't a single building in sight. Mitch turned onto a two-lane road, and within seconds the downpour curtained off any sign of the interstate in Kate's side-view mirror.

With no streetlights or oncoming headlights to break the gloom, they might have dropped into another dimension. Kate didn't realize she wasn't breathing properly until the truck slowed further and jounced onto an unpaved side road marked View Turnout.

Realizing Mitch must intend to park here, she took in a shuddering gulp of air. This wasn't exactly a campground, but it beat blundering around in zero visibility.

They climbed until the road ended at a rock formation. An overhang cut the steady thrum of rain to a slow trickle.

Mitch peered into the thin area of gray defined by the headlights. "At least we've got some shelter. This doesn't look like a canyon mouth, and we've come uphill a little."

"So we're not likely to wash away?" Kate asked.

"That's true." He killed the motor and turned off the lights. "Well, honey, we're home."

She started to laugh. Then she remembered that, tonight, there would be no motel and no sleeping outside.

She had no choice but to share the camper with Mitch.

Chapter Seven

Mitch had intended to fetch an umbrella from the camper, but Kate apparently didn't hear his instructions to wait in the cab. Instead, she jumped down at the same time he did, and they both arrived at the back soaking wet.

He tried to shelter her as he unlocked the door. Standing so close, it was impossible not to notice the way the dampness brought out the perfume in her hair and the musky allure of her skin.

Mitch scolded himself for getting distracted again. He'd been thinking about Kate this morning, wondering if she might have bailed out on him overnight, and that was why he'd forgotten to lock up properly.

Absentmindedness could be deadly for a man in his situation. He needed to concentrate, all the time. Including now.

As soon as he did, he realized he should use some of the large rocks lying about to wedge the truck's wheels. The grade here was so uneven that a small mudflow might send them slipping down the slope.

"Get inside," he said. "I'm going to shore us up."

"I'll help." Without waiting for a response, Kate stepped into the rain.

A steady stream of water ran from the brim of Mitch's hat, but at least his head was dry. "You're not dressed for this."

"Then we'd better hurry, hadn't we?" she said.

He had to admire Kate's zeal as she rolled and lugged rocks beneath the tires. Within minutes, her clothing was soaked, but she hardly seemed to notice.

Mitch noticed. Wet clothes didn't leave much to the imagination, and Kate's compact figure had curves in all the right places.

With her blond hair sticking to her face and her blouse and jeans molded to her body, Kate bore little resemblance to a crisply efficient school principal. She looked more like a—well, a temptress.

He couldn't help imagining how it would feel to press his lips to hers and cup those soft, tantalizing breasts in his hands. He could imagine the shudder that would run through her, the way it had when they'd touched by accident.

Mitch wrenched his thoughts back to the present. "We've done as much as we can out here."

"Do you think we're safe now?" she asked.

He nodded toward the rocks wedged beneath the wheels. "Safe from a minor mudslide, anyway."

Inside the camper, Kate wrapped her arms around herself and smiled at him apologetically. "I guess I'd better change. I'm kind of a mess."

He removed his hat, patted the felt with a towel and set it crown-side down so it wouldn't lose its shape. "I'll make tea. After you change, you can wrap up in a blanket if you're still cold."

"What about you?"

"I'll change, too."

Mitch didn't take chilling lightly. A guy who tried

to tough it out on the range not only risked catching pneumonia, he ran the more immediate danger of hypothermia.

Kate rummaged through her suitcase and he turned to the stove. Locating a pot and filling it with water got his mind off her for about thirty seconds, until she brushed by him on her way to the bathroom.

In the narrow space, her body fit much too snugly against his. He became intensely aware that the two of them were alone in the wilderness, stripped of the trappings of civilization.

Gritting his teeth against the masculine tightness in his groin, Mitch angled away and let Kate pass.

"Sorry." She slanted him a look that was half apology and half speculation.

But not invitation, he reminded himself as she vanished into the bathroom. Even if she wanted him, and he suspected that on some level she did, she belonged to someone else.

Moose might not deserve her; a mental image of that man touching Kate filled Mitch with dismay. But she'd made her choice and her commitment, and he respected it.

After lighting a burner, he got out two chipped mugs, a tea bag and packets of sugar. A gust of wind hit the side of the camper, jolting it so that Mitch nearly dropped one of the cups. Water pelted the roof with such force that they might as well have parked beneath a cascade.

He didn't want to spend the rest of his days in a rattletrap camper, battered by the elements. He wanted a home and a woman as spirited and intelligent as Kate, but free to love him.

Under normal circumstances, he would have found

a wife of his own by now, he mused as he removed his boots, stripped off his soaked garments and replaced them with a nearly identical shirt and pair of jeans. He'd put his future on hold until the day he got the High C back, but that day had never come. Maybe now it never would.

He hung his wet clothes from hooks attached to the walls. Not that there was much hope of anything drying with the air so humid.

The door to the bathroom opened and Kate edged out. She had towel-dried and fluffed her hair, and put on a rose-colored sweater that made her skin glow. Everything about her looked soft and touchable.

The water began to simmer, and Mitch dunked the tea bag in it. He needed to keep his hands busy and his mind focused.

Kate squeezed by him in a cloud of teasing perfume and yielding body parts, and moved toward the small table. "This is cozy."

Way too cozy. His whole body was vibrating with excess coziness. If they got any cozier, he might explode.

Kate curled onto the padded bench behind the table. She fit perfectly in the Lilliputian setting. She would fit just as perfectly in his arms, and his bed, Mitch thought.

"The camper suits you. It's kind of small for me, but I try to keep my clumsiness under control." He was pleased at how normal he sounded. Also by the fact that he'd managed to say anything remotely intelligible.

"Actually, you move with a lot of grace for a man."

He couldn't formulate a response that didn't involve

offering to show her exactly how graceful he could be, so he went back to dunking the tea bag. The water was nearly black by now.

"Tell me about Flagstaff," Kate said. "Exactly who or what are we going to see?"

Mitch seized upon this change of subject with relief as he filled their mugs. "Old Doc Rosen died at his cabin in Oak Creek Canyon south of town, as I mentioned."

"How long ago?"

"About thirteen years. I hadn't seen him in a while, but it felt like the end of an era." He set out a bowl of sugar. "Doc delivered me at home, and he treated me as a kid. I even came back my freshman year in college to consult him when I got bronchitis."

He could see the doctor's face, its high forehead wrinkling with concern, the wide-set eyes full of wisdom. Then he realized his memory must be playing tricks, because he could swear the man was a dead ringer for Raymond Burr.

"You mentioned his daughter."

Mitch handed Kate her mug. "She's an artist. I think she used to teach at Northern Arizona University, which is why Doc moved to that area when he retired. Also, he loved the scenery. According to Doc, Texas was too flat."

He described how he'd tried to reach Sarah Rosen after Billy Parkinson showed up with the papers, but there was no phone at the cabin.

He'd finally driven to Arizona, only to learn that she and her husband were in Europe. A renter at the cabin had let him take a look around, but he'd found nothing useful.

The management company had said Sarah and her

husband moved frequently. He wrote to their most recent address, but his letter came back. He obtained a new address and wrote to that, but never received a reply. Several additional letters either went astray or were ignored.

"I suppose a detective could have found her." Mitch sat opposite Kate, careful to keep his legs from touching hers. "But by then I was going to law school and struggling to keep my head above water."

She stirred sugar into her tea. "Wouldn't your Dad's bank have some record of his checks? He might have paid off the loan that way."

"Dad liked to pay cash for things," Mitch said. "He did make regular withdrawals, but they could have been to pay the ranch's expenses."

Kate started to say something, then stopped. From her embarrassed expression, Mitch could guess her thoughts.

"And it's possible he really didn't repay the loan," he concluded. "But that would be completely unlike my father."

"Maybe he couldn't," Kate said. "This doctor probably wouldn't have pressed him, but—possibly he was getting confused in his last years. Maybe he signed the quitclaim without understanding what it meant."

Mitch had been over this territory endlessly in his mind. "I can't imagine that he would have been allowed to sign a document if he was that far gone. Sarah could tell us for sure what her father's mental state might have been."

"And you think she's returned by now?" Kate murmured, her tone gentle.

Mitch realized he was stirring his tea so hard it had

slopped over. He set the spoon down and folded his hands on the table. "I called the management company last week, before I went out to the ranch to meet Billy. I was hoping to get enough information to twist his arm, maybe force him to back down."

"They said Sarah was home?" she asked.

"Not exactly," Mitch admitted. "They said she'd terminated their services a few days earlier, that she was planning to sell the place."

"They didn't have a phone number for her?"

He shook his head. "But she could be staying at the cabin."

"Do you think she might have heard about you shooting that cowboy?" Kate asked. "What if she's told the police you might come looking for her?"

He thought about the winding road that led to the cabin. "We could be trapped," he conceded. "If you'd like me to drop you in Flagstaff and collect you on the way out, I'll be glad to."

She set down her cup and glared at him. "Mitch Connery, it was just speculation. Besides, you need me."

If she only knew the half of it! "Do I?"

Kate's face scrunched like a kid's as she pondered. Watching her was an entertainment in itself. "First of all, if Sarah *is* there, she's less likely to panic if you come with a woman."

"Possibly."

"And since you've already visited the cabin once and didn't spot anything useful, maybe you need a second set of eyes."

"Considering that you couldn't see three armed thugs in the middle of the street, I'm not convinced you'd be much help in that department," he said drily.

She appeared on the verge of a sharp reply, when her outrage melted into a chuckle. "It's only a problem if I get dust under my contacts. But I don't care if I have to blink and blear my way through that canyon, I'm coming with you!"

If fire had shot from her ears, it wouldn't have surprised him. The woman could be fierce when aroused.

He wondered what she was like when aroused in a different way. He couldn't allow himself to touch her physically, but an urge swept over Mitch to sing to Kate.

During his college days, he'd noticed the effect his voice had on women. He had only to pull out his guitar at a small gathering and begin to sing, and they gravitated toward him, entranced.

Not that he expected Kate to respond that way. She wasn't an impressionable coed, and he wasn't trying to win a date for the evening. But he found himself wanting to share this private aspect of himself.

Besides, a little diversion would help to pass the time. They were stuck here for the rest of the day, and two people could only play cards for so long.

Mitch reached into a nook for the guitar case.

NO ONE HAD SUNG to Kate since she was a child. That was not counting the time at a park concert when Moose got drunk and decided to treat the band as his personal karaoke accompaniment.

He hadn't exactly been singing *to* Kate, but at her. The *Gazette's* editor, in a tongue-in-cheek review, had written that, as singing, it might make Caruso turn over in his grave but that, as an imitation of a cow with digestive problems, it ought to win a blue ribbon at the next state fair.

She stretched out along the couch as Mitch bent over the guitar like a father cradling a baby. A peep from the pitch pipe got him started, and then he tuned each string in turn, tightening the pegs as he checked and rechecked the harmony.

Kate's body responded as if he were stroking her instead of the instrument. Each arpeggio became a massage; with each twist of a peg, his fingers seemed to probe and ease her sore muscles.

The thrum of rain outside and occasional gusts of wind rocking the truck heightened her sense that they had taken refuge together. As long as they huddled close in their cocoon, she had nothing to fear.

Mitch began with an old Don McLean song, one of Kate's favorites, "And I Love You So." His fingers rippled across the strings and his unhurried baritone filled the empty spaces of her heart.

The words about a man who has survived loneliness and found love seemed to well from deep within him. He gazed into space, only occasionally noticing the placement of his fingers.

Kate couldn't move and she didn't want to. It was impossible to separate the rich timber of his voice from the emotion that wrapped around her. Mitch might be lost in his music, but he was lost in it with Kate.

She had gained the sense, almost from the moment they met, that he was a man forced by fate to be solitary but who was by nature capable of great warmth. Now she couldn't help picturing him as master of his own hearth, tenderly sharing it with his family, protecting and nurturing them.

Kate had never been the sort of woman who sought a protector, or who believed in head-over-heels passion. She didn't need to be wooed with bouquets of roses; she could grow her own.

But suddenly she wasn't sure she wanted the man who shared those roses to be Moose.

The realization startled her. When and why had she begun doubting her plans for the future?

"What are you thinking about?" Mitch murmured as the song ended.

"Roses," she responded distractedly.

The chords rippled, and he segued into "The Rose." It was followed by melodies from Celine Dion and Elton John and then a catchy Caribbean number from Harry Belafonte, with the pelting of rain providing a percussion background.

Kate released her disturbing thoughts. She was far away from Grazer's Corners. Everything would look different when she got home.

The last piece he sang was "The Music of the Night." The melancholy half-light in the camper fused with the music to form long, shivering shadows in Kate's soul.

Yet she felt no fear of the darkness, only a sense of longing for something she had never known. Something that might already have passed out of reach.

Mitch's voice touched and caressed her, and she savored every rich note of it. As he murmured the sensual lyrics, her lips tingled, and heat flowed to her core, and her breasts felt ripe, as if ready for harvest.

Kate didn't know herself. She ought to be frightened, perhaps even repulsed by the wanton way her eyes feasted on Mitch's hands, and on the muscles bulging in his forearms as he strummed.

But she wasn't. For one liquid, silvery space in time, caught in the stream of her own awakening sensuality, she lost all sense of duty and order. It was inconceivable that nature would create such splendid vistas inside her, without good reason.

The last note vibrated away so slowly that she couldn't tell when it ended. Then there was nothing left except the pelting of rain, not a single whisper of music to ease the tension charging the air.

Mitch lifted his head, and their gazes met. She read an invitation, and knew that if she didn't answer, her desire would answer for her.

But she must not make such a decision now, seduced by song and accidental intimacy. If she could only force herself to be strong, this weakness would pass, and then she would remember that this was not the place where she belonged, and this was not the man she belonged with.

Her thoughts must have shown in her face, because Mitch moved away to set the instrument in its niche. He kept his face averted until he returned with a deck of cards and a blank expression.

"Sorry, but this is the only other form of entertainment we've got," he said as he shuffled deftly. "Lady's choice. What shall we play?"

"Anything but Hearts," she said.

MITCH SPENT AN uneasy night dozing on the unfolded couch, which must have grown new lumps since the last time he'd checked it. Above on the bed overlying the truck cab, Kate should have had a more comfortable rest, but he could hear her tossing and turning.

They'd strayed dangerously close to the fire today. He had watched her slowly ignite as he sang, and it had taken all his strength not to put the guitar aside and take her in his arms.

And he would have taken her, given the slightest encouragement. Thank goodness she had held fast to her standards.

Mitch Connery wasn't a callous seducer who could steal a bride from her wedding, make love to her and then abandon her. But he was wanted for murder. He could make no promises now.

And even if that weren't so, he couldn't give up his ranch and follow Kate back to her hometown, which he suspected would be necessary if he were to keep her.

A ranch wasn't just a piece of land, or a way to earn an income. It formed a living, breathing entity, an entire world of people and animals. They were born and grew and loved and lost within its boundaries, and then bequeathed their hopes and challenges to the next generation.

He could be happy with that sort of life, hard as it might be. But he doubted Kate ever could.

By midmorning Wednesday, the rain slacked off enough that they dared return to the freeway. It worried Mitch that the Tiny Wheeler Gang had such a big head start en route to Santa Fe, and he didn't want to waste any time.

The spirits must have been conspiring against him, however, because on the outskirts of Kingman, the troublesome left front tire blew itself to smithereens. Only a firm hand on the wheel and a lot of luck enabled him to jerk the truck onto the shoulder without serious damage.

Kate sat frozen in her seat, where the belt secured her in place. She hadn't spoken much in the past twenty-four hours.

"You all right?" In case she hadn't grasped the fact, he added, "We blew a tire."

Her eyes came into focus, as if she had just landed in the present after a long flight of fancy. "What do we do now?"

He watched the passing stream of traffic for a police car. The last thing they needed was to attract friendly attention that might turn hostile. "Change it as fast as possible."

"You've got a spare?"

He shrugged. "I've got a hollow piece of rubber that passes for one."

Fortunately for them, no one stopped. The town was aswarm with travelers en route to the Grand Canyon, so it was unlikely a casual passerby would notice or remember his out-of-state plates.

For the third time in nearly as many days, Mitch donned a pair of coveralls and set to work. After putting on the spare, it took several hours to locate a new tire of the correct size, which Kate paid for, and get it mounted and balanced.

Mitch had to admit, he didn't know how he would have survived this latest setback without the lady's help. He had fled Texas with a few hundred dollars in cash, all he'd been able to take out of his ATM. Gas, food and campground fees had eaten most of it, and he didn't dare advertise his whereabouts by withdrawing any more money.

He would repay her, of course. A Connery always honored his debts. But had Kate not been along with her handy plastic money, he doubted the tire dealer would have taken a scribbled IOU based on nothing more than the word of a defrocked Texas rancher.

They passed another uneasy night, although at least

this time they had the benefit of an RV camp with hookups. The camper's water tank needed refilling and its battery recharging, and once again Mitch reluctantly let Kate pay the bill.

He was accustomed to silence and to his own thoughts, but her withdrawn air bothered him on Thursday as they drove to Flagstaff. The air was crisp and pine-scented on this plateau, and they could see snow-covered peaks in the distance, but she seemed oblivious to the spare beauty of the high desert.

"What's going on?" Mitch said.

"Excuse me?" She'd worn her glasses today, and they gave her an endearingly owlish aspect as she turned toward him.

"You've been freezing me out ever since my serenade." He moved into the slow lane to let an oversize motor home with blue racing stripes rampage past at well over eighty miles per hour. "Is my singing that bad?"

She gave him a rueful grin. "It's wonderful."

"Having second thoughts about the rest of our journey?"

She shook her head.

"Help me out here," Mitch said. "Is this some female thing you don't want me to know about?"

Kate frowned. "Female thing? Like what?"

He didn't know exactly what he meant, except that in his limited experience women frequently disappeared into rest rooms while making vague references to "girl stuff." "I don't know. PMS. Smeared makeup. A run in your panty hose. Whatever." He wished with all his heart that he'd never brought the subject up.

"You know what?" Kate said. "You're blushing."

That made him even more self-conscious. Mitch couldn't figure out why he'd tried to pry into her ruminations in the first place. She was probably figuring out new and humiliating ways to punish delinquent students and presumptuous cowboys.

"I guess it's none of my business." He exited the freeway and found himself on the old Route 66. "You hungry?"

"Starved."

"Let's pick something up." It was early afternoon and Flagstaff, despite its modest population of around forty-five thousand, had enough fast-food eateries, trendy cafés and foreign restaurants to feed five times that many people.

"First an ATM."

Mitch stopped near a sign advertising the Pine Country Pro Rodeo, and Kate withdrew money. Then they treated themselves to Chinese food, eaten in the camper by the side of the road.

"Where to next?" she asked when she came up for air.

Mitch had been studying his map. "We'll swing south on State Route 89 toward Sedona. That'll take us through Oak Creek Canyon."

She nodded and went back to eating. But, although he loved Chinese food, Mitch found he wasn't hungry. It was because of what lay ahead, and what he might, or might not, find at the cabin.

Even though the most serious problem facing him was the murder charge, more than anything he wanted the High C back. And he might not get it. Not now, not ever.

In the back of his mind, the idea had been building for the last year or so that the key must lie with Sarah

Rosen, or in the cabin where Doc had died. There must be something he had missed during his previous trip.

Mitch recognized that at some level he'd been afraid to go back. Afraid he would find the cabin sold and remodeled, or maybe even learn that Billy Parkinson really had taken over the loan.

They finished eating and set out south from Flagstaff. Kate no longer appeared so preoccupied; instead, she was paying close attention to their surroundings.

"Some of these senior citizens are a real menace," she observed as a truck pulling a silver trailer whipped past them. "Did you see the guy at the wheel? A little wizened fellow wearing goggles and grinning like he was driving the Indy 500."

"He won't make very good time," Mitch observed. "In a guzzler like that, he'll spend half his trip in the gas station."

"And make up for it afterward by driving like a maniac." Kate sighed. "Speaking of maniacs, I wonder where those bandits are."

"Well ahead of us," he said gloomily.

THE PREOCCUPATION that had descended upon Kate for the past two days had lifted abruptly. She wasn't sure whether Mitch's awkward questions or their arrival in Flagstaff deserved the credit, but it was a relief.

She had been replaying her reactions to Mitch over and over in her mind. It was hard to admit, at thirty-one, that she'd never considered herself a sexual person not because she wasn't but because she'd never been truly aroused.

Kate expected herself to anticipate situations like this. She'd been primed for her wedding night, and then swept into a romantic semiabduction by an alluring man. No wonder she felt like an autumn leaf about to lose its grip on the branch.

She'd been struggling to get the upper hand over her susceptibility. That was proving difficult. Every time she glanced at Mitch, she noticed some new and intriguing detail—the way the sun had bleached the hair on the back of his arms, or how appealingly his amber eyes darkened when he frowned.

But now that they were less than an hour from the cabin, nervous excitement hummed through her. She wondered whether Sarah might be there, and what she would say. Besides, who could waste time worrying when they were passing through some of the most spectacular scenery on earth?

On either side of the narrow canyon loomed cliffs of blazing white, yellow and red. Gorges slashed the bluffs, and atop a rise she spotted a twisted rock formation that might have been sculpted by Martians.

Oak Creek might not compare to the Grand Canyon, which lay some eighty miles to the north. But here the scenery felt close enough to touch and far more pristine.

According to information on the back of the map, this road had begun as a cattle trail. Before that, Native Americans had lived throughout the area, fishing in the creek and raising corn, beans and squash.

Beside the road ran the creek bed, splashing along a boulder-strewn course and occasionally widening into pools. Kate wished she had time to stop and go wading.

She also wished that crazy man pulling the silver trailer had stayed ahead of them. Instead, he must have pulled over or taken a wrong turn, because he was behind them again, riding on their bumper.

With a grimace, Mitch steered as far as he could onto the shoulder, and the old geezer swooped by. Right behind him came a motor home painted with blue racing stripes. Kate glimpsed the driver, a large grizzled man with wisps of white hair sticking out beneath his golf cap.

"Two of a kind," Mitch muttered. "They've both passed us before, and here they are again. With any luck, they'll keep each other busy playing road tag and stay out of our way."

"If they keep passing each other, they might hit oncoming traffic," Kate said.

"What would you suggest we do? Make a citizen's arrest?"

"Someone ought to." Ahead, the vehicles vanished around a bend. The road's downhill slant only added to their speed. "But it won't be me."

She remembered that day in Grazer's Corners—could it be scarcely over a week ago?—when Moose had joked that she should give the van a ticket. She'd been so angry about getting elected sheriff that she'd confronted the occupants just to prove she could handle them.

Who had she thought she was? Kate wondered. She didn't want to be sheriff; she just wanted to do the best she could for the students at her school.

People told her that, in partnership with her teachers, she had worked wonders in bringing order out of chaos. To Kate the real miracle wasn't the rising test scores; it was the joy she felt every time she made a difference in a young life.

"Well, look at that." Mitch pointed ahead. The

truck-trailer and the motor home had stopped at the edge of the road. The two white-haired drivers stood shouting and waving fists at each other.

There was no oncoming traffic, and Mitch drove by cautiously. Kate didn't see any sign that the two RVs had hit each other, but tempers were boiling over and perhaps radiators were, too.

"Those boys need to grow up," she grumbled. "I'd have them each write an essay on the need to slow down and smell the roses. Then I'd make them take a refresher course in driver's ed."

"It might also help if someone pointed out their liability should they cause an accident," Mitch agreed. "They could lose everything they own."

"Spoken like a lawyer."

"Sorry."

The altitude was dropping sharply, Kate realized as her ears popped. "Are we getting near the cabin?"

"Just a few more miles." The words came out tightly. "We'll have to keep our eyes peeled for the turnoff. It's easy to miss."

The road curved again. The canyon was so narrow here, Kate doubted it measured even a mile across.

As they cornered, she spotted a dirt road a quarter of a mile ahead. "Is that—?"

From behind a boulder emerged a rusty brown van. It lumbered across the highway and halted, blocking their path. To their right lay a sheer rock face; to their left, the creek ran close by the road.

They had driven into an ambush.

Chapter Eight

Two of the bandits burst from the van, shotguns in hand. Despite their masks, Kate could see that the tall, lanky one was grinning.

White-hot fury boiled through her. She hated leering Dexter Dinkens and—what had Mitch called the short thin guy with the cold eyes?—oh, yes, Nine Toes Blankenship. And big hulking Tiny Wheeler, sitting behind the wheel.

"Get down on the floor!" Mitch barked as he snatched his gun from beneath the seat.

Kate fumbled with her shoulder belt. Before she could get it off, she heard a sound like thunder behind them. In the road, the two bandits looked up, puzzled.

Dropping the gun, Mitch put the truck into gear. He yanked the wheel to the right until they pressed so close to the rock face she could have reached out and touched it.

Ahead of them, the van spun backward, its wheels kicking up loose gravel as it retreated toward the boulder. Gaping in confusion, Dexter performed a dance of indecision. Nine Toes stood his ground.

"Hang on." Mitch pressed Kate against the door. "Whoever's coming might clip us."

Her fingers dug into the armrest. Yet, oddly, she felt no panic. Mitch's body was like a shield, sheltering and guarding her.

It awakened sensations that she had fought ever since he sang to her. Now, with fear forcing them close, she discovered that her efforts had been futile. She wanted him so much her bones ached.

In the side-view mirror, she glimpsed the motor home with blue racing stripes, coming around the corner. Alarm flashed across the driver's face as he stomped his brakes.

Shifting her gaze to the road ahead, Kate caught a series of images, each as distinct as a photograph: Dexter diving for the creek; Nine Toes accidentally firing his gun at the ground, then hopping for safety; and the motor home skidding sideways amid the scream of ripping metal.

A split second later, the silver trailer rounded the bend, jerked and bucked, then fishtailed madly. Eons passed as vehicles slid, tilted, crunched, groaned, and finally came to rest in a tangled heap.

Mitch's body over Kate's allowed only intermittent glimpses of the wreckage. When at last silence fell, he sat up and started the truck.

"What are you doing?" she gasped.

"Getting out of here." He edged back onto the road. "With any luck, they're too dazed to notice which way we're headed."

Kate's back stiffened. "We can't leave the scene of an accident! What if people are injured?"

A jerk of his head indicated one of the RV drivers climbing out of his cab. "He looks mobile enough. I don't see any fire and nobody's been crushed. If they were wearing their seat belts, they should be shaken up at worst.''

"What about those two bandits?" she demanded. "They weren't inside vehicles."

"This highway is patrolled pretty regularly." Mitch steered through a clear patch of roadway toward the turnoff. "Besides, one of these guys must have a..."

From down the canyon reverberated the *scree-scree* of a siren.

"Guess somebody heard the crash," Mitch said.

Kate dropped her objections. With police on the way, Mitch needed to make himself scarce in a hurry.

"Do you think the bandits will report you?" she asked as they jounced from the pavement onto a rutted side road.

"If we're lucky, they'll be too busy thinking up lies about why they were toting those shotguns and blocking the road." Mitch guided their rig uphill until a clump of pines screened the highway.

His words failed to reassure Kate. "Is there another way out of the canyon? I can't imagine having to return this same way. It's like a trap."

"There may be an alternate route from the cabin to the highway. We'll still be in the canyon, but at a different point. And it should be dark in a little over an hour." He shrugged. "I'm willing to take my chances. What's the alternative?"

Once, at a Las Vegas convention, Kate had balked at trying the slot machines. Now she was playing a game where the stakes were infinitely higher.

But as Mitch said, they didn't have much choice.

NINE TOES'S FOOT HURT like fire, but he'd be danged if he'd say anything to those Department of Public

Safety troopers. Like as not, they'd haul him off in one of their big white cars to some hospital or other.

What he wanted was to get up the trail and nail Mitch Connery before the varmint skedaddled. Nobody killed one of Nine Toes's pals and got away with it, even if Jules *had* been setting a trap.

They'd called in from Albuquerque, only to have Billy order them back here. Dexter had groused the whole way, saying he figured Loretta kind of fancied him and he thought she would come real quietlike, maybe even help them catch that no-good cousin of hers.

They knew where she was staying. She'd charged the motel bill on her credit card and Billy had tracked it through his computer.

But back they'd come, and the job would be well and truly done by now if it wasn't for those two road-hogging senior citizens. The geezers were glaring at each other from opposite sides of the road, each one complaining loudly to the troopers.

"Hey!" Tiny Wheeler hulked alongside him. "Man, you stupid? Hide the durn gun!"

Nine Toes started to sidle behind the rock and then thought the better of it. "My foot's kinda sore. I reckon I stubbed it."

With a look of disgust, Tiny grabbed the shotgun and headed for the van. A moment later, he returned empty-handed. "Where's Dexter? He still hiding in the crick?"

"He gave up on that." Nine Toes pointed to where Dexter sat on a rock, trying to wring out his clothes, which wasn't easy because he was still wearing them.

"At least he had the sense to ditch his gun," muttered Tiny.

"Ditch it?" growled Nine Toes. "He's so yellow, he prob'ly lost it runnin' for cover."

"Here's the deal," said Tiny. "Anybody asks why we stopped, we hit some kind of animal, like an armadillo or a coyote. We figgered we ought to finish it off. That'll explain the guns, too, iffen anybody mentions 'em."

One of the DPS troopers sauntered toward them. "Either of you fellas need medical attention?"

They shook their heads.

"Who was driving?"

Tiny cleared his throat.

"Could I see your license, sir?"

The trooper took Tiny aside to get his account of what happened. That was when Nine Toes realized he had to speak to Dexter before the cops got to him.

No telling what that idiot might say. One hint that they'd been laying an ambush and they'd be searched, manacled and strung up.

Nine Toes waved at the gangly kid on the rock. No response. For some reason, even a simple arm gesture made his foot hurt worse, which got him mad at Dexter. Finally he yelled, "Hey, you young fool, git over here!"

The kid came loping across the highway, where cars and RVs had begun backing up. The trooper was busy directing traffic, which had to squeeze through the single open lane.

"Hey," said Dexter when he arrived. In wet clothes, he looked like a scrawny chicken. "While them cops is busy, why don't you 'n' me take the van up the road and finish the job?"

Nine Toes decided the kid wasn't entirely stupid.

They had Mitch boxed in, and who knew when they'd get another chance?

Of course, the cops might hear the shots. Also, he and Dexter couldn't exactly drive away without anybody noticing.

He was weighing the possibilities when a whole wave of pain rolled upward from his foot. It hadn't hurt so bad since the time he shot his toe off.

That was when he realized he hadn't just stubbed it. With a curse that would have made his mama come after him with a paddle, Nine Toes stared down at the blasted remains of his boot.

"Well, dang," he said. "I musta been in shock."

"Sir?" It was the trooper again. "You're bleeding. You need to see a doctor."

He sure did. He no longer cared if they ever got Connery cornered, or whether they made it to Santa Fe, or even if Loretta preferred a scatterbrained young'un to a seasoned rangehand. He just wanted some doc to put him out of his misery.

"Naw, he ain't no sissy," he heard Dexter say.

Didn't that just beat all? "Iffen you like it so much, next time you shoot…next time a truck runs over your foot, we'll tell the doc to stay on home. Then ever'body can call *you* Nine Toes."

"But that's your name," protested Dexter.

"Not no more it ain't," said Eight Toes, right before he passed out.

DESPITE A BRILLIANT sunset slashing the sky, the canyon lay in shadow. The road angled up a rocky slope toward a clump of cypress trees, but for the moment only the twilight provided cover.

At any moment, Kate expected to hear sirens gaining on them. But she detected nothing beyond the rumble of overheating engines below, echoing off the bluffs.

"What a mess." Looking down, she could see a traffic jam, the smashed RVs and a clutch of emergency vehicles with lights flashing. "I hope no one's hurt."

Mitch kept his gaze on the path. "It's a miracle there was no explosion."

"Do you think Tiny Wheeler will give us away?"

"Considering how many shotguns he's carrying, I expect he'll want to attract as little law-enforcement attention as possible."

He guided the truck around a rutted, sloping bend. Runoff had washed out the shoulder and the slightest skid would have sent them tumbling, but Mitch kept a steady hand on the wheel.

Through the open window, a breeze played through his shaggy hair. His confidence, and his air of being at home out here, melted the tension from Kate's muscles.

She recalled the heat that had flooded through her in the moments before the crash. But the stimulus hadn't just been physical.

Mitch's first instinct had been to protect her. It was his caring, and his courage, that had energized her, not merely the powerful impression of his chest and hips and arms. On the other hand, she wouldn't mind experiencing that same contact again under less stressful circumstances.

"Kate?" At a level spot sheltered by a boulder, he halted the truck.

"Is something wrong?"

"You tell me." Gold-flecked amber eyes examined

her. "You just went through a traumatic experience. Ever since, you've had a funny expression on your face. Do you feel okay?"

She managed a weak smile, relieved that he hadn't been able to guess her thoughts. "I do feel kind of shaken."

He reached for her arm and laid it across his thigh. Warm fingers pressed her wrist and she realized he was taking her pulse.

"I thought you were a lawyer, not a doctor," she said.

"On a ranch, you've got to know a little bit of everything." He checked his watch. "It's elevated a little, but that's okay." He didn't let go of her hand, though.

Silver glimmered through Kate's veins. Despite the sounds of doors slamming and horns honking that drifted up from the highway, she didn't want to move. Ever.

She could feel every sinew and muscle in Mitch's thigh. She heard the deliberateness of his breathing and knew desire was growing in him.

This awareness of him as a man rippled through Kate, changing her in subtle and sparkling ways. She wondered if Mitch could see the glow in her skin. Even without looking in a mirror, she knew it was real.

Reluctantly, he removed her arm from his lap. "We need to go on."

She nodded, afraid to speak. There was too much that might slip out, perhaps even a dangerous admission that could change her life forever.

Kate couldn't keep lying to herself. She hadn't simply been keyed up by her expectations of a wedding night. The truth was that Mitch awoke sensations in her that Moose never had, and probably never would.

Yet she was determined not to act on them. The discovery of her own needs didn't mean that she had stopped being Kate Bingham.

She was still the principal on whom her school depended for its fragile, newfound return to high academic standards. She still loved her students, and her staff, and her hometown and the life she had built for herself.

It was a life that Moose, and only Moose, could share.

They were rumbling on their way. The moment had passed. Maybe, she thought with the tiniest glimmer of hope, the subject would never come up again.

In the midst of the cypress trees, they found a clearing studded with weathered stucco buildings connected by covered patios and archways. It didn't resemble a cabin so much as a small outpost.

As he switched off the engine, Mitch nodded toward a building in the back. "There's no water or power lines up here. Everything's trucked in, dug up or generated on the premises."

"Seems like a lot of trouble. I don't see why anyone would want to..." Kate turned to open her door and for a moment forgot to breathe.

Through a gap in the trees, the earth spread out before her like a newly discovered planet, primitive and achingly raw in the purple dusk. Kate had the sense that prehistoric beasts still stalked these buttes, and that civilization remained a distant and uncertain possibility.

"That's why," Mitch said, and got out of the truck. She dropped to the ground. The isolation of this place was almost overwhelming, yet the glory of it dazzled her.

Then, in the distance, a hot-air balloon danced above the canyon, its red, blue and yellow stripes a cheeky contrast to the red rocks. The sight of it jolted Kate back to reality. They had a mission to accomplish, and time was short.

She turned her attention to the premises. If people lived here, they didn't put much store in landscaping. There was nothing but moss and a few scrubby bushes.

They had just reached the porch when the door opened. The movement was so unexpected that she missed her step and had to touch Mitch's arm for support. Her cheek grazed his shoulder, and she inhaled deeply, braced as much by his subliminal essence as by the solid feel of him.

A woman emerged, fortyish, her gray-streaked dark hair pulled back and fastened with a clip. An embroidered vest topped a white blouse and jeans.

"Hello?" She blinked at them. "What's going on? I heard an awful racket down…" Recognition dawned. "Mitch Connery!"

From her expression, Kate couldn't tell whether the woman wanted to hug him or call the cops. One thing, at least, was clear: They had found Sarah Rosen.

DOC'S LIVING ROOM might be small and the furniture shabby, but there was a *National Geographic*-quality view through the picture window, Mitch reflected during a break in the conversation. He hoped the doctor had finally managed to exorcise the flatness of Texas.

"I'd take any reasonable offer for the place," Sarah said as she served iced tea. "It's a great place to paint, but I can't make a living doing that."

She had explained, once they got past the initial greetings, that her husband had died several months ago. A self-employed international business consultant, he'd left her with no insurance and a son in college.

Although she had found a teaching position at a private college in Phoenix, it didn't pay very well. The cabin must be sold.

Sarah had aged markedly in the fifteen years since Mitch last saw her. Grief and time had darkened circles beneath her eyes and etched wrinkles into her forehead.

He wished he could help her, for Doc's sake as well as her own. But right now he was in no position to help anyone.

"I'm sorry about not answering your letters," she said. "After I got the first one, I tried to find out what had happened to the loan papers. If they'd still been here when Dad died, that would prove the quitclaim is a forgery. But we moved so much that mail went missing a lot, and Dad's housekeeper was hard to track down. I don't even know how much the loan was for."

"Thirty thousand dollars," Mitch said. "That much I do remember."

She sat on a wicker chair and hooked one heel over a rung. Despite her current difficulties, there was still a brightness to Sarah's face that reminded him of the energetic young woman who used to design floats for Gulch City's annual Fourth of July parade.

"Dad left a lot of books and magazines and papers when he died," Sarah continued, "and I could only stay a short time. The housekeeper had to sort things as best she could."

"His death was written up in the *Gulch City News*,"

Mitch recalled. "Billy must have seen it. Since he'd worked for Dad, he knew about the loan."

"I never liked that man," Sarah said. "Dad didn't, either. I know he wouldn't have sold Billy the loan. In fact, he'd eventually have torn up the papers even if it hadn't been repaid. But I doubt he realized they were still here. Dad was pretty casual about loaning money to friends."

"Was he getting forgetful?" Kate asked. "Could he have signed the quitclaim without realizing what it meant?"

Sarah shook her head. "Not in my opinion. But I couldn't prove it in court."

"Did you ever find the housekeeper?" Mitch asked.

"I finally found out she's living with her son in Mexico," Sarah said. "She wrote me that a man came by who said he was a lawyer, and took some papers. Well, there *was* a lawyer in Sedona who settled Dad's estate, but I don't think he ever drove out here."

"Could she identify Billy in court?"

"Maybe," Sarah said. "But she's pretty old. I don't know if she could make the trip."

Mitch could see how much it bothered her, not being able to help. "Don't worry about it, Sarah—it probably makes no difference. The only courtroom I'm likely to see is the one in which I'm tried for murder."

He had told her when they arrived about Jules Kominsky's death. He didn't want Sarah to find out about the murder charge later and believe he'd been trying to hide it. Thank goodness she'd believed in his innocence without question.

Kate, who had been listening intently, leaned forward. "This might be relevant to your defense, though, don't you think? If you can prove that Billy went to such lengths to defraud you of the High C, that might make a jury more likely to believe he would set you up to get killed.''

The point was well taken. Mitch had been thinking like a rancher, not a lawyer.

Besides, although they seemed to have reached a dead end, he felt an itch, the kind that refuses to go away, to put his hands on something tangible in this cabin. ''Are there any papers or records left? Maybe there's something Billy overlooked.''

Their hostess got to her feet. ''There's a safe in the back. I left some odds and ends in it, since we were moving around so much.''

The two women preceded Mitch from the room. Although Sarah was taller, Kate's swinging stride and authoritative posture gave the impression of greater height.

On their way through the house, he glanced into a couple of bedrooms. Bright serapes draped the walls, and multicolored rugs splashed the tile floors. Even in twilight, the house felt light and airy.

They entered a room lined with empty bookshelves. Sarah opened a closet and switched on an interior light to reveal the outline of a built-in safe.

Mitch wiped his hands on his jeans. They'd gone clammy on him, and his throat had tightened.

There had to be something inside, some clue, some new lead. As Kate had pointed out, not only the ranch was at stake. He would need every possible bit of evidence to clear himself of the murder charge.

Mitch hadn't allowed himself to dwell on the negative, but now he admitted silently that even Loretta's testimony might not be enough to free him. A prosecutor would paint her as biased in his favor, perhaps even willing to lie on his behalf. He needed evidence of Billy Parkinson's true character.

Kneeling, Sarah fiddled with the dial. She swore a couple of times at its obstinacy, before it finally creaked open.

From inside, she retrieved a sheaf of papers and a leather-tooled box. When she carried them out and spread them on the desk, they made a pitifully small pile.

"A lot got thrown away, or maybe Billy took off with it," Sarah apologized, dusting her hands. "Here's Dad's will, leaving everything to me, and a copy of his last income tax form."

With her permission, Mitch flipped through the rest. There was a home insurance policy, the deed to the cabin and other personal papers. "What's in the box?"

Sarah unsnapped the lid and showed them. "His wedding ring. His captain's bars from the army. A silver-and-turquoise tie clip Mom gave him for their twenty-fifth anniversary. And this." She held out a worn blue bankbook stamped Bank of Gulch City.

Mitch accepted it gingerly. His fingers felt clumsy as he opened it. Inside was Doc's full name, Myron Schwartz Rosen, and a list of handwritten deposits and withdrawals.

The last entry, a withdrawal, had been made fifteen years ago. The balance was seven dollars and fifty-three cents.

"I'm not sure why he left the account open," Sarah said. "I kept meaning to close it, but I was always too busy, and that's not enough money to worry about. It's probably been confiscated by now, or whatever Texas does with unclaimed accounts."

Mitch stared at the yellowing pages. Leaden disappointment weighted his chest.

For years he'd tried to find Sarah, and he'd dragged Kate through an ambush to get here. All for nothing. Whatever evidence Doc might have left when he died, Billy must have taken it.

"Was your father a careless man?" Kate asked. "Did he usually leave business unfinished?"

"Not really." Sarah refolded and stacked the other documents.

"Then he may have had a reason for leaving the account open," she said.

Mitch's brain churned into motion. Kate could be right. Maybe there *had* been some activity in the account that didn't appear in the book. "You mean my father might have been making payments into it?"

Excitement flickered across Sarah's face. "I never thought of that! Probably part of the loan was paid off before Dad retired, but there could have been a balance left."

"Dad would have kept paying on it, even after Doc Rosen retired," Mitch said. "Possibly even after your father died. He'd have figured that eventually the account would go to you."

"If we can prove your father was making payments and they aren't reflected in the loan papers that Billy has..."

"...then we can make a strong case that the loan papers are outdated, and probably null and void," Mitch finished. He remembered a couple of points from his lawsuit. "Billy's never produced any record that he paid your father for the right to take over the loan. Also, he didn't file the quitclaim until two years after the date Doc Rosen supposedly signed it. Add the facts together, and the weight of the evidence could shift to our side.''

The three of them exchanged glances. They seemed to share the same exhilaration, but also, he suspected, some wariness.

It was Sarah who gave voice to her doubts. ''On the other hand, maybe Dad just left the account open as kind of a sentimental gesture, a tie to his old home-town. Maybe the loan had been fully paid before he left Gulch City. If it was, I don't know how we could prove it.''

For once, Mitch hoped his father hadn't been too quick to settle a debt.

KATE HUNG ON TO the armrest as they bumped down the trail in gathering darkness. This was an alternate route, one that met up with the highway farther along and should bypass the jam.

She wondered why Tiny Wheeler and his gang hadn't come up the hill to the cabin. Maybe they'd been arrested, or injured in the crash.

Mitch had warned Sarah of possible danger, and she'd left a few minutes before they did, to spend the night in Sedona. By following her, Mitch had pointed out, they could make sure she didn't get stuck some-where in the dark.

A thought that had been tickling the back of Kate's brain for hours finally popped into the forefront. ''You know, Tiny Wheeler and his gang should have been nearly to Santa Fe by now. I wonder why they came back.''

''Getting rid of me must be their first priority.'' Mitch slowed as a jackrabbit fled through the glare of his headlights.

"Yes, but why would they come back on the outside chance that you'd stop at the cabin?" Kate mused. "If we'd gone straight on, they would have missed us entirely."

Mitch's eyes narrowed. "Somebody must have tipped them off."

"It couldn't have been Sarah. She wouldn't have deliberately turned us in," Kate continued. "And anyway, she had no idea we were coming."

"Did you tell anyone?"

She was about to shake her head, when she stopped. "I mentioned to Moose that we were going to see someone in Oak Creek Canyon. I just wanted him to understand why it was taking so long."

Mitch gave a low whistle. "He's the mayor, isn't he? With no sheriff around, he might have taken a call from Chief Novo."

Kate shivered. This ambush had been her fault. She'd given away information that could have gotten them both killed.

It wasn't fair to blame Moose. If the Gulch City police chief asked him for information, he would have no reason to hold it back.

He didn't understand the situation, and she knew she couldn't convince him of the truth long-distance. From now on, it might be safest if she didn't contact him at all. Until now, Kate had felt certain she would be back home within a few days, and that life would go on as planned. But long miles and a deep emotional rift were widening the gap between her and the world she had known.

The truck jounced as they moved onto the highway.

In the dark, she couldn't see much beyond the patch of roadway directly in front of them and, above the ebony cliffs, a cold, star-tossed sky.

She had never felt so far from home.

Chapter Nine

It was dark by the time they circled back to Flagstaff via the interstate. Mitch pulled into the first RV park they saw and, exhausted, Kate fell asleep almost instantly.

She awoke to find him dressed and making toast. He stared out the camper's tiny side window with narrowed eyes, as if peering ahead to Santa Fe, and didn't turn when she skimmed by on her way to the bathroom.

As she closed the door behind her, Kate registered the fact that he had his Stetson in place. The man was ready for action.

When she emerged, her coffee and toast had been set on the small table. Mitch leaned against the sink, lost in thought.

Morning light played across the planes of his face and raised golden highlights in his hair. The deep Texas tan testified that neither law school nor exile had made him any less a cowboy.

Where were his thoughts? At the ranch that he might never reclaim? With Sarah as she struggled to survive widowhood and financial setbacks? Or ahead, where the Tiny Wheeler gang might be laying yet another ambush?

Kate sipped her coffee and wondered when she'd become so involved in a stranger's world. Or when her own world had begun to seem as if it belonged to a stranger.

For the first time in her life, the cozy illusion labeled *future* had blurred. She could no longer picture Moose's house filled with her furniture, or the little boy who resembled him and the girl who looked just like her. Those children had been so much a part of Kate's mental landscape that it was hard to believe they had never actually existed.

Instead, she kept seeing her kitchen with its old-fashioned stenciled flowers, and Mitch sitting there polishing his boots. Every detail of the scene had been engraved in her memory with shining clarity. But that wasn't the future either, she reminded herself, just a brief moment in the past.

After Mitch resolved his legal problems, she would return home to a town that hadn't changed. She wasn't sure how she was going to respond to all those people who expected her to be the same old Kate Bingham. But if she wasn't the same person, who was she?

The foundation that steadied her was, as always, the thought of her work.

Each of the returning students held a special place in her heart. And, in a few months, there would be a new crop of kindergartners with scrubbed, open faces.

Kate had been given a gift. It was the gift of seeing individual needs without losing sight of the whole structure: curriculum, staffing and physical setting.

She had already made a difference in many lives. But there was more to do, and the gains could easily be lost. When the first bell rang the Wednesday after Labor Day, one thing was certain: Kate Bingham would be there. The new one *and* the old one.

Mitch removed the dishes as soon as she was done. "Time to hit the road."

"Think we'll make Santa Fe by tonight?" she asked.

"Good Lord willing and the creek don't rise," he quoted an old saying.

"Then we'd better get started. I hate rising creeks."

MITCH STEERED EAST across the high desert plains. Rocky and harsh, the land guarded ancient secrets: the ruins of prehistoric Indian dwellings as well as a vast meteor crater and lava tubes left by long-silent volcanoes.

Quite a few travelers turned off at the exit for the Petrified Forest and Painted Desert.

Mitch had no interest in sightseeing. He had wasted too much time already.

The bankbook burned in his pocket. It might be the key to recovering the High C and perhaps, he hoped, one of the keys to his redemption.

Loretta, the only honest witness to the shooting of Jules Kominsky, was the other.

He wished he had gotten to know his cousin better. In his memory, she remained a gawky teenager with curly chestnut hair and clear eyes that came to life when she rode horseback, or when she sang.

If only Mitch had explained to her about his legal problems with Billy Parkinson and how he was trying to solve them, maybe she wouldn't have taken matters into her own hands. True, then he might have had no witness at all to the fact that he had acted in self-defense, but he would prefer that to risking his cousin's safety.

Yet here he was, risking Kate's safety. She could have been killed in the ambush yesterday, Mitch thought.

Reluctantly, he allowed himself to steal a sideways glance at her.

One elbow on the lip of the window, she sat with chin in hand, studying the severe sweep of land. Sunglasses masked her eyes.

Unlike his cousin, who at twenty-five was still dewy with inexperience, Kate understood the dangers and was prepared to face them. She had come on this trip of her own free will, Mitch reminded himself.

He tore his attention away. He must not allow himself to dwell on her compact figure and the curve of her mouth. He particularly did not want to remember how soft and yielding she'd felt when he arched over her yesterday, bracing for the impact of the RV.

Even after he fell asleep last night, his senses had carried her imprint. It had overwhelmed his dreams, in which fiery shotguns and careening trailers vanished to leave him and Kate magically alone.

Alone, with his body cupping hers. Alone, with her blue eyes widening as his hands traced along her rib cage to the small, firm breasts. Alone, when his mouth came down on hers and her tongue licked fire into his soul.

Swallowing a groan, Mitch gripped the steering wheel and squinted into the harsh light. It was well past noon and they were nearly to New Mexico.

"Hungry?" He hoped she would attribute his ragged tone to weariness.

The sunglasses swung toward him. "Starved."

"Not too many places to eat around here," he admitted, almost sorry that he'd brought up the subject. "We could make sandwiches."

Kate winced. "The fridge is empty." She'd fixed a hurried meal of odds and ends the previous night and, he now recalled, had mentioned something about stopping by a store this morning.

"We'll be in Gallup in less than an hour," he said. "Plenty of places to eat there."

Kate nodded. "Let's restock the glove compartment while we're at it. There's something to be said for junk food."

Ten minutes later, Mitch spotted a turnoff and an oversize sign announcing a trading post. In the hopes that the store sold food along with Indian crafts and souvenirs, he headed down the ramp.

A scattering of vehicles punctuated the gravel parking lot, including two beefy motorcycles. There was no sign of the rusty van.

Mitch wondered if Tiny Wheeler's gang had gotten ahead of them. With luck, they might have been detained by the police, but he wouldn't count on it.

When they entered the trading post, they discovered that it comprised one huge ramshackle room stuffed with postcards, headdresses, moccasins, beadwork, pottery and bumper stickers bearing mottos from the amusing to the annoying. A section at the back formed a small dining area.

Mitch followed Kate to a cracked plastic booth. They both ordered grilled cheese sandwiches for speed's sake.

He tucked his menu away behind the salt and pepper shakers and surveyed their fellow diners. A couple of senior citizens sat absorbed in each other.

Two muscular young men sporting tattoos dominated another booth. Seated beside them were two
women with long stringy hair and maroon windbreak-
ers. These, he assumed, were the bikers.

Many motorcycle clubs these days raised money for
charity. These two couples weren't wearing charitable
expressions, however, so Mitch averted his gaze to a
scenic wall calendar, on which the days had been
x-ed out.

He took a second look. "Damn."

"What?" asked Kate.

"Did you know today was Friday?"

"Well, yes, but I didn't see what I could do about
it."

He gave her a halfhearted smile, then lapsed into
gloomy silence. They wouldn't arrive in Santa Fe until
late. Since he gathered the Pocket Opera Company
wasn't actually in production yet, it most likely closed
on weekends.

It might take until Monday to find Loretta. Mitch
only hoped Tiny Wheeler had no more information
about her whereabouts than they did.

The cheese sandwiches arrived slightly burnt. Mitch
exchanged glances with Kate, shrugged and ate.

Since he preferred not to have to stop again in Gallup, they picked up some canned goods in the trading
post's mini-mart. They exited into the glare of afternoon light and the roar of revving motorcycles.

Kate winced at the noise. As they strolled toward
the truck, Mitch caught a sneer on the face of one of
the bikers. Evidently the guy had noticed Kate's reaction, because he twisted his throttle even harder.

Mitch recalled their earlier conversation about macho men who felt compelled to flex their figurative

muscles at any provocation. Apparently they had stumbled across just such a Neanderthal specimen.

Kate was picking her way cautiously across the gravel, paying no attention to the bikers and lagging behind Mitch. Shifting the groceries to his left arm, he reached to unlock the back of the camper.

The other motorcycle vroomed to the edge of the road. Mr. Macho jerked his throttle a few more times while his stringy-haired lady wrapped her arms around him.

Then his bike shot forward. It circled too close for comfort, spewing gravel that narrowly missed Kate.

Mitch fought down the impulse to get in the truck and teach the man a lesson about playing chicken. That was a great way to attract the attention of any passing police officer. Besides, it would mean stooping to the jerk's level.

Despite a beckoning gesture from the other biker, Mr. Macho wasn't ready to leave. He swung around again, and Mitch saw the lady on the back shouting in his ear, egging him on.

"Kate!" He thrust the sack into the camper and turned toward her. If only she would take refuge between the truck and a parked car! Instead, as the motor noise intensified, she swung around, folded her arms and glared at the biker.

Oh, Lord, she was playing principal of the world again! As he lunged toward her, Mitch's thoughts flashed back to the first time he'd seen her, standing in front of Harmon's Department Store lecturing the Tiny Wheeler gang about seat belts.

Even then, he'd known she was someone special, if slightly crazed. That was before he'd fallen in love with her. Before he'd—*what?*

The bike leaped toward Kate. Mitch didn't believe the cyclist actually intended to hit her, but he couldn't take that chance.

He reached her with a split second to spare, caught her by the upper arms and thrust her out of harm's way. At the same time, the biker whipped the motorcycle around, sending a spray of gravel slashing across one side of Mitch's face.

He stumbled and fell painfully onto one knee. The cycle skidded sideways across the lot, raising shrieks from the female rider as Mr. Macho fought to keep from dumping them both. They came to an angled rest within a few feet of a parked RV.

The older couple emerged from the trading post and strode toward them. "Are you folks all right?"

The driver yanked his bike upright and let out a string of curses. The couple stopped in their tracks.

Mr. Macho's ashen-faced companion had no choice but to hang on as he wheeled the bike around and shot toward the street. They and the other couple vanished in a cloud of exhaust fumes.

"Do you need some help, sir?" asked the white-haired man.

Mitch's leg hurt and the side of his face felt as if a puma had raked its claws across it. He dusted himself off and straightened his hat. "I'm fine."

"You're bleeding." It was Kate, at his side. "Mitch, I'm sorry I acted like an idiot. Thanks for saving me...again."

Worry shone in her blue eyes, and, in the turmoil, a rebellious hank of blond hair had fallen over one cheek. But she was safe and whole, this small, feisty, insane woman.

When he saw her in danger, the truth had forced itself dead center into Mitch's brain. He loved her.

But he couldn't have her. He was in no position to offer her a home or a family or a future. Besides, she belonged to someone else.

"You should go inside," the older woman said. "They must have a first-aid kit."

The last thing he needed was to have people fuss over him. "We've got one in the camper," Mitch managed to say.

Kate gave the pair a warm smile. "Thanks, but I can take care of him."

As the couple walked away, Mitch knew he ought to get moving, too, but his legs were trembling. Kate helped him as far as the camper's steps, where he sat heavily.

"You're stunned," she said. "Do you feel cold?"

"Just shaky. It'll pass."

Something red dripped across his line of sight. Blood. Absentmindedly, he reached up to wipe it off.

Kate grabbed his wrist. "Go ahead, rub dirt into it. That ought to help."

"Sorry." Mitch tried to think clearly. "The first-aid kit is under the sink. Get me patched up and let's push on."

"To where?" Kate demanded.

He couldn't believe she'd forgotten. "Santa Fe."

"In your condition?" She edged by him into the interior. "Here's the plan." The cabinet door squeaked open. "I patch you up. I drive to Gallup, we find an RV park, then I cook us a delicious meal of— what did we just buy?—corned beef hash and lima beans."

He hated to lose the time, but his entire side was

stiffening where he'd fallen. There was no way he could drive to Santa Fe tonight.

The truck was cranky and capricious and, burdened with the camper, it required an experienced hand even in daylight. Kate could manage as far as Gallup, but he didn't want her taking it any farther, especially not after dark.

Two more cars pulled into the lot. "Let's get going before anyone else asks questions," Mitch said. "Just give me a clean rag to wipe my face. You can make me beautiful later."

Behind him, an intake of breath indicated she was about to argue. Quickly, he added, "We can camp in Gallup if you insist. Just hurry."

"All right, tough guy." Kate emerged with the first-aid kit and a cloth. "Promise me you'll slather some antibiotic cream over it, too. I'll do the rest when we get there."

"Much appreciated," said Mitch.

By the time they reached a campground nearly an hour later, he could barely move his leg, despite having downed several ibuprofen pills. Kate helped him inside, opened the couch into a bed and eased him onto it.

Her cool hands moved across his face, wiping off his hastily applied lotion and replacing it with a fresh dressing. Mitch felt safe in her care.

He also felt stupid. He had escaped a death trap in Texas and dodged bullets in California, only to let some punk get the better of him in the middle of no-where.

"Let's see the rest of the damage." She indicated his leg. "Do you want me to cut off your jeans, or are you going to take them off yourself?"

He couldn't resist a crooked grin, even though his face felt like hardened plaster. "Honey, you can undress me anytime."

"I'll slit 'em." She glanced toward the kitchen counter. "Where do you keep the scissors?"

"Never mind." With a low groan, he reached for his heavy belt buckle. It slid open with the greatest of ease, as if to mock him with the reminder of how its cantankerousness had ensnared Kate in the first place.

Except that, right now, he wasn't so sure which of them had been ensnared. Not when he could only push his jeans halfway down, and then had to pretend not to notice while Kate stripped them the rest of the way. It was maddening the way she did it, with the detached efficiency of a teacher examining a child who'd been hurt on the playground.

How could she stay so cool when his body was throbbing with her nearness? It was diabolical, this feminine imperviousness to the silken whisper of skin against skin as her hand caressed his bare thigh and knee and calf.

Mitch could feel his bruises purpling, but oddly, it didn't hurt even when Kate began applying hydrocortisone cream. Two forces stronger than pain were warring within him: exhaustion, and a powerful swelling in his groin. He was thankful for the protective covering of his extralong shirt.

Had it been any other woman attending him, he would have fallen asleep the minute he stretched out. Now delicious fingers of desire crept along his midsection. Couldn't Kate sense his response? Didn't she feel a quickening in her own body?

He wondered if the time would ever come when he could tell her that he loved her. He thought about telling her now, but first it was imperative that he...that he...fall asleep.

KATE AWOKE AT MIDNIGHT on her bed above the cab. Below, she heard Mitch tossing and turning on the couch.

Praying that he wasn't developing an infection, she climbed down and touched his forehead. It felt damp but cool.

She sat beside him, too restless to go back to her own bed. Although she had pretended indifference this afternoon, touching him had stirred her in unexpected ways.

Her flesh felt highly sensitized just being beside him. The man was hard, and yet a vulnerability lurked beneath his toughness.

Kate studied the bandage strips crisscrossing his cheekbone and forehead. Without thinking, she bent and brushed her lips across a patch of uncovered skin.

A drift of fragrance, so faint it was almost below the conscious level, percolated into her veins. At the same time, Mitch sighed and shifted position, dislodging the covers from one hip.

His injured leg lay bare. In the dim light, Kate couldn't see the bruises. Tentatively, she feathered one hand along his knee and thigh. Just to check for swelling.

She didn't find any. What she did find were corded muscles that tensed instinctively beneath her touch.

A wave of pure, hot desire rocketed through her. Her throat clenched as she became fiercely aware of how much she wanted him. But how could she respond this way, when she was going to marry Moose?

Perhaps these sensations sprang at least partly from

the elemental excitement of a woman who sees a man thrust himself protectively in front of her. Like a knight from the Middle Ages, Kate mused. One of Agatha Flintstone's Norman conquerors, perhaps.

She had always found the town clerk's fantasies amusing, but now she found them reassuring. Her feelings were normal. Instinctive. Universal. They had less to do with Mitch Connery as a real, flesh-and-blood man than with archetypes and legends.

The thought of Agatha steadied her. Kate smiled at the memory of the town clerk whacking Tiny Wheeler with a book as he ran through the church.

It was amazing how the townspeople had rallied in the face of danger. Especially Charity Arden and her amazing aim. The thought of her old friends comforted Kate, and she tugged the blanket into place over Mitch.

What had been going on in Grazer's Corners while she was away? Jordan Grazer would be marrying Randall Latrobe tomorrow. Kate hoped they had worked out whatever seemed to be troubling Jordan.

Then, next weekend, big blond Garrett Keeley and slender, elegant Hailey Olson would walk down the aisle. She had never seen any longing gazes or stolen kisses exchanged between those two, but surely they knew what they were doing.

The way she had, Kate mused. She'd been so certain she knew what the future held for her. Now...well, now she couldn't think past getting Mitch safely through the night.

Rolling onto his stomach, he muttered something incomprehensible. Maybe he was developing a fever after all, even if it wasn't detectable yet, she thought anxiously.

It might be best if she lay down beside him. The opened-out couch was wide enough for two, and this way she was more likely to awaken if his condition worsened. That confusing rush of longing had abated, and she felt fully in control of herself.

After fetching her pillow, Kate slid under the covers beside Mitch. His warmth enveloped her, and although she shrank as far to one side as possible, her leg brushed his lightly furred calf.

Certain that she wouldn't sleep a wink, she nestled into place and closed her eyes. The next thing she knew, she came awake with the vague sense that time had passed, although it was still dark.

Beside her, Mitch moaned. The sound startled Kate, until she remembered that she had chosen to sleep beside him in order to keep tabs on his condition.

His forehead still felt cool, but the moan indicated he might be in pain. Quietly, she got up and padded to the sink.

Returning with a cup of water and two pain pills, she managed to get them down the man. It was amazing that he could swallow them while still half-asleep. She wished she had the same facility.

Kate put the cup away and returned to bed. This time, sleep refused to come for a long time, and when it did, it was filled with haunting legends and tantalizing archetypes that looked exactly like Mitch.

IN HIS DREAM, he lay injured on a battlefield that resembled a gravel-strewn parking lot. Beside him knelt a blond nurse, her blue eyes alive with concern, her hands deft and gentle.

When she touched him, the pain eased, and the ground beneath him transformed itself into a grassy field. He felt her stretch out beside him and realized this must be a form of New Age healing.

That seemed odd, since he had the impression he'd been fighting in the Civil War. But the pieces of the dream shifted and fell into place, so that in a subliminal way it all made sense.

Mitch knew instinctively that this woman, this healer wanted to raise the power of his life force. She must not realize that his life force had already raised itself.

Slowly he reached out to touch the smoothness of her uniform. As he did, he became aware of the fresh herbal scent of her hair and the almost unbearable nearness of her hips to his.

The nurse couldn't have known how long it had been since this soldier had lain with a woman. Not since his law school days. Law school? But if he wasn't a soldier, he must be Mitch. And this woman was...

Kate. His Kate. Good Lord, what was she doing in bed with him?

Mitch opened his eyes to the glow of early dawn. The half-light turned the camper's interior to a rosy haze.

He lay on his side, half-covering Kate with one knee and his arm. Her filmy nightgown scrunched about her waist, and the sheets had been kicked away.

A long, shuddering breath escaped her, and then her eyes blinked open. They widened at the sight of him, and Mitch swallowed, preparing to make awkward apologies. Also, he ought to move away. But he couldn't.

She lay motionless for a long moment, absorbing

the situation. He felt her shift beneath him, but she didn't draw back.

Instead, she reached around him and traced the bare skin of his back. Her hands feathered down to the elastic on his waistband, stopping as his body tightened.

Moving closer, she brushed her lips across his cheek, tentatively at first, then with greater daring. Neither the early-morning stubble nor his disheveled state fazed her as she nibbled his jaw.

With exquisite gentleness, Mitch ran his thumbs from her waist up to the small, shapely breasts. The peaks strained beneath his touch, and he bent to take them in his mouth, one after the other.

Kate gasped and arched against him. One knee rubbed his thigh, and he could feel heat blazing through her.

He wanted her so badly he could hardly restrain himself. He forced himself to pause. This moment was too precious to rush.

Then, ignoring the lingering soreness in his muscles, he lifted himself above her and leaned down to let his tongue trace the line of Kate's throat. Her hands gripped his hips, bringing him once more to the edge of an explosion.

Not yet. Not yet.

He tasted her lips, and then her temples, while his thumb teased the tips of her breasts. She was so small that he could completely cover her, yet she filled his horizon.

Kate curved against him, her body rubbing sinuously so that she touched him everywhere in turn. Her satiny skin grazed the hardness of his thighs and chest in open invitation.

A man could hold out for only so long. With the relieved sense of entering a place where his entire soul yearned to go, Mitch stroked her legs apart and eased himself into her.

He felt a momentary resistance and heard a soft cry from Kate. Before he could register what it meant, she pulled him more tightly into herself, thrusting against him until she drove all rational thought from his mind.

IT SEEMED INCREDIBLE that Kate had never put the pieces together before. Now, in one burst of revelation, she saw that she had never been indifferent to sex; she had simply never truly understood what it was.

She shouldn't be doing this with a man who wasn't her husband, but she might as well command her heart to stop beating. Mitch took her elusive, fragmentary longings and fused them into a white sword of desire.

From the moment she felt his body covering hers, Kate had been lost. Her breasts were on fire, and a deep hunger welled inside her.

When he took her virginity, there was a twinge of discomfort. It melted instantly into a great aching need that only he could relieve.

She felt his power and strength flowing into her. With every tormenting stroke, he gave her more of his masculine essence.

This cowboy, this untamed male, was losing himself in her. Kate had never felt so alive. Her body buzzed as if electricity flowed from his arteries into hers.

For this moment, Mitch belonged entirely to her. She gripped his buttocks, and relished feeling his thrusts simultaneously within herself and outside, through her hands.

He drove harder, all the ferocity of his nature unleashed in this one act. Elation bubbled within Kate, intensifying until she could no longer think but only yearn, profoundly and desperately, for him to propel her with all his force into a new dimension.

At the same time, she relished the moments when he stopped and let the longing build in them both. The ragged need made his blazing reentry even more delicious.

How incredible that these sensations had lain buried inside her, unsuspected, for so long. This was all she had imagined a wedding night could be, and more.

Again Mitch paused. Kate caught an impression of the whole man, from his rumpled hair down the length of his body, from his careless youthful days on horseback to the tempered hardness of the adult, poised to give himself to her.

He would hold nothing back. And neither could she.

Then he filled her. And filled her again, moving faster and faster. She clasped him and gave him back all of herself.

With a final thrust, they merged and, for one shimmering moment, hovered above themselves, blending together in body and in spirit.

As fire muted into afterglow, Mitch relaxed to one side and gathered her close. Kate lay against his chest, happy to have this quiet spell. Happy to inhale his scent and listen to his regular breathing.

But not yet ready to look into his eyes. Not yet ready to deal with the fact that her neatly ordered life had just fractured into a thousand glittering shards.

Chapter Ten

Mitch prided himself on being able to size up a situation quickly. Whether it was a distant slithery motion on the range that marked the path of a rattlesnake, or a slight misstatement that indicated a client might be lying, he seized on it instantly.

Well, he hadn't been very quick on the draw this morning. It had never occurred to him that a woman as sophisticated as Kate could be a virgin.

He had taken that from her. With her consent, of course, but that didn't lessen his obligation.

Beside him, she propped herself on one elbow. "Do you have some kind of postgame ritual that I should know about?"

"Excuse me?"

"You don't smoke, so I don't think you want a cigarette." It was amazing how young Kate looked in the dawnlight. Young and serious. Between her eyes, a tiny pucker had formed, and her full lips pursed in concentration. "Do you need to exercise? Or tune up the truck or something?"

"Are you under the impression," Mitch said, "that men indulge in some kind of primitive, individualistic rite after making love?"

Kate's cheeks colored. "Well, that's what I've heard. You know, girl talk. And I've read about it, too."

"Where?" he asked. "In health education manuals?"

"Agatha Flintstone loaned me one of her novels," Kate admitted. "I guess I shouldn't generalize based on gossip and a single book."

"What exactly did this hero do?" Mitch asked. "Smoke a cigar with his toes?"

She laughed. "No, he was a knight. I think he got up and sharpened his sword."

"Mine's sharp enough already, thank you."

"I'm well aware of that." A contented sound escaped her.

Slipping an arm around Kate, he pulled her against his shoulder. A sweep of blond hair curtained her face, until she pushed it behind one ear. She looked as comfortable as a cat dozing before a fire.

"Do you understand what..." He stopped himself. "Of course you understand what we did."

"Oh, we're going to have *that* discussion." Kate sighed. "I'm not sure I'm ready to deal with it."

Mitch wasn't sure he was, either, but he'd never been the sort of man to shirk his responsibilities. "It was your first time."

She nodded.

"How long were you engaged?" he asked.

"Years and years," she said. "I was saving myself." That made him feel worse, until she added, "I guess I was saving myself for you."

That sounded wonderful. If he hadn't been a fugitive, and if he'd been able to offer her the kind of life she wanted, Mitch would have whisked her to the nearest justice of the peace. "Kate, you realize..."

"That it wouldn't work? Yes," she said. "I could never be happy on a ranch. And you could never be happy anywhere else."

He sat up, and wished he hadn't. In the fires of passion, he'd managed to overlook the great throbbing misery of his injuries. Gritting his teeth, Mitch pressed on. "There could be other complications."

"Such as getting shot?" she guessed.

"That isn't what I meant." He didn't want to spoil this special moment together any more than she did. But she might have to deal with the consequences when he, willingly or not, was long gone. "Has it occurred to you that you might be pregnant?"

Her lips formed a small O. Then she said, "Mitch, I was supposed to get married on Saturday."

"So?" he said.

"Moose and I wanted to get our marriage established before we had a family," Kate said. "I've been taking birth control pills."

It was his turn to say, "Oh."

"So you don't have to worry about that," she reassured him.

He wasn't really worried. In a way, he was sad. A pregnancy would have forged a lifelong link, although, if Chief Novo had his way, Mitch's life might not last very long.

Because time was short, and because the opportunity might not come again, he wanted to tell Kate that he loved her. If only he could believe it wouldn't distress her to hear it. "Kate..."

As if eager to cut short the discussion, she tossed back the covers and hopped out of bed. "You have to be hungry. We never did manage to have dinner last night. How about some corned beef hash?''

"I... Fine. Whatever you want." Regretfully, he watched as she moved toward the bathroom, her nearly transparent nightgown teasing him with little glimpses of flesh along the way.

You're mine. I've claimed you and I'll never let you go. That was what he wanted to say. But Mitch had to let Kate go, if that was what *she* wanted.

He had never believed in the selfish proposition that life was meant to be easy. Sometimes joy walked hand in hand with pain. He was grateful for the joy. He just hoped he could bear the pain.

IT WAS HARD to shower in the tiny space. Kate found she had to slip her clothes and towel out the door, lock herself in and then use the entire bathroom as a shower stall.

Thank goodness she'd managed last night, with help from the campers next door, to get hooked up to the park's electrical connections and water supply. Now a hot spray sluiced over her, luxurious and refreshing.

As she soaped up, Kate still couldn't believe she had just made love to Mitch. Even more, she couldn't believe she had no regrets. Surely Moose deserved better treatment than this.

Her shampoo made the whole room smell like honey and clover. As she lathered it in, Kate remembered the song from *South Pacific* entitled "I'm Going to Wash That Man Right Out of My Hair."

But exactly which man was she washing out?

Mitch's sense of honor might make him offer to marry her. Also, Kate knew that he did care for her. But she surely wasn't the wife he dreamed of, a woman who would happily spend her life lassoing cows and repairing fences.

As for herself, she found Mitch exciting and magical and dashing, all the things a woman dreamed about. But when it came to choosing a husband, Kate needed not an adventurer but a man whose way of living was compatible with her life's work.

She had heard of people requiring a last fling to remove their doubts. Maybe that was what this whole experience amounted to: preparation for marriage to the right man.

And no matter from which angle she examined the subject, the logical choice was Moose. She would have to confess to him. In turn, she expected him to come clean about his own premarital activities.

It would be a test for them both. But if Moose proved to be the kind of man who loved her enough to forgive, maybe…

Kate finished rinsing out the shampoo and turned off the water. Even in the steamy room, the air felt suddenly cold. But not any colder than reality.

Who was she kidding, anyway? she wondered as she cracked open the door and retrieved a towel. How could she ever be happy with Moose, after what she'd experienced with Mitch?

Still, she had to face the fact that she and Mitch could never make a life together. She was thirty-one years old and she wanted a home and children. To get them, she would have to be practical.

But first, she needed to help save the man she loved from an unjust fate. Whatever it cost, Kate would stay the course until he was proved innocent. She owed him, and her heart, that much.

After that, well, she would have to make some definite decision about Moose. She already had a notion of what that choice would be, but it wasn't in Kate's nature to be hasty.

While her fingers were still slick from the shower, she slipped off her engagement ring and tucked it into her cosmetics bag. She could always put it on again later.

THEY TRAVELED EAST to Albuquerque and then northeast, reaching Santa Fe before nightfall. Mitch insisted on driving most of the time, although Kate relieved him occasionally.

They found a spot at a well-appointed RV park in the northern part of town. The desk clerk told them that in another two weeks when the tourist season reached full swing, they'd never have gotten in without a reservation.

Kate ran laundry while Mitch stocked up on groceries and called Information. He returned disgruntled. "I found the number for Pocket Opera but their answering machine says no one will be there until Monday. There wasn't even an address listed."

"There must be stores in town that carry musical instruments." Standing in the middle of the laundry room that adjoined the park office, Kate transferred a load into a dryer. "They should have information about a new opera company."

"Good idea," he said, pacing. "I'll get the yellow pages, and let's check them out."

Kate squinted at her watch. The dryness and the seven-thousand-foot altitude, combined with her contact lenses, were making her eyes tear. "At six o'clock on a Saturday night? You really think anybody'd be open?"

"We have to find her!" Red marks stood out where he'd removed his bandages.

"We're both falling apart," she stated firmly. "I vote we have dinner."

Reluctantly, he conceded the point. They soaked in the hot tub while the laundry dried, then grilled fish and vegetables on an outdoor barbecue.

The air filled with aromas from neighboring cookouts as well as their own. As they ate at their picnic table, Kate could hear snatches of conversation in English, German, Spanish and an Asian language she guessed might be Japanese. Soft laughter drifted through the twilight.

For this moment, the residents of this camp formed an informal community. She wished she could meet some of the others and hear their stories.

Mostly, she wished this time could last forever, sitting across from Mitch, watching his enjoyment of their meal, feeling a tingle run through her when their gazes met.

After a while, they carried their dishes inside, then went to collect the laundry. While folding it inside the camper, they kept bumping into each other until finally they gave up, tossed the clothes in the basket and made love.

They never even noticed that they'd forgotten to eat dessert.

ON SUNDAY MORNING, while waiting for the stores to open, Kate and Mitch walked through the town's scenic central plaza, the heart of the original settlement that dated back to the early 1600s.

It was lined with shops selling artwork and Indian crafts, but Kate was most interested in the Spanish architecture. They strolled by the old cathedral and, a few blocks away, the mission of San Miguel.

Reluctantly, she let Mitch escort her back to the truck. They headed for their first destination, a store selling instruments and sheet music.

The shop was airy, with handmade drums and flutes for sale along with conventional instruments. A bulletin board announced concerts, performances and the upcoming season of the well-established Santa Fe Opera.

Finally Mitch spotted a small, handwritten notice about auditions for the new company, with an address on Paseo Peralta. He copied the number and they hurried out.

It was easy to locate Paseo Peralta on the map. However, after driving along it for several blocks, they began to find the street numbers confusing.

Kate checked the map again and discovered that the road looped around town. Finding the audition site would be a long, slow process in this heavy traffic.

And so it was. They passed the state capitol, innumerable shops and the post office before they finally discovered the building on the opposite side of town from where they'd started.

The small adobe structure was locked tight, and the parking lot empty. A sheet posted on the door listed the audition schedule for the following day.

L. Blaine would be making her appearance at 2:00 p.m.

AS HE PULLED the pickup into their camping slot and killed the engine, Mitch felt frustration roar inside him.

His cousin was here in this city. At this very moment, she might be window-shopping in the plaza or hanging out at a coffeehouse.

If he drove for just a little longer and looked a little harder, maybe he'd find her. After all, how many people could there be in Santa Fe?

He knew he was kidding himself. First of all, it would be an incredible piece of luck to find Loretta by chance. Secondly, his cousin might be naive but she wasn't stupid. Whatever reason she'd had for running away, it would be enough to make her lie low in Santa Fe.

Mitch swung down from the cab with his usual carelessness, then fought not to groan aloud. How could his leg still hurt so much when all he'd done was dodge a motorcycle?

Angry at himself for his weakness, Mitch limped around to hold the door for Kate, but she'd already gotten out. Judging by the expression on her face, she hadn't missed a single wince as he rounded the truck, either.

"I'm a little stiff," he explained. "I need some exercise."

"What you need is another soak in the park's hot tub." Her glare cut off his protest. "You're not going to do yourself or Loretta any good if you let pride turn you into an invalid."

To his surprise, Mitch didn't want to argue. The thought of the whirlpool spa was too tempting.

And he wanted to spend time with Kate. Not just making love, much as he relished that experience, but talking and being together.

The irony, he reflected as he unlocked the camper and stood back to let her inside, was that in his rush to clear his name, he was also hastening the moment when he would lose Kate forever.

Might lose Kate forever, he amended, gritting his teeth and climbing the camper's rear steps. He wasn't ready to write off the possibility that when she visited the High C, when she saw its raw beauty and how much Mitch belonged there, she might decide to stay.

Grandma Luisa had given up an opera career to marry Sam Connery. Mitch knew such ideas were old-fashioned and, besides, there was some truth to the story that Grandma had been fleeing tyranny in her homeland.

But if true love had once conquered all, surely it could happen again.

In the camper, Kate pulled her suitcase from beneath the couch and rummaged through it until she found her swimsuit. Then she eyed Mitch before saying, "I don't suppose I need to change in the bathroom any more, do I?"

"Not unless you're hiding something I haven't seen yet," he drawled.

She chuckled, closed the blinds and began unbuttoning her blouse. Mitch knew he ought to get out his own swimsuit, but he was enjoying watching her. She glanced up, caught his eye and turned an intriguing shade of pink.

That was the nice thing about blondes, he reflected. They couldn't hide their blushes. On the other hand, Kate was one of the few grown women around who still had the delicacy to blush at all.

"I think I could live without an audience," she said.

"Do I detect a note of sarcasm?" Mitch angled himself against the counter and waited.

"Maybe I *will* go in the bathroom."

"You'll have to pass me first," he taunted.

She tried to frown, but it didn't take. "You planning on going in the water with your clothes on?"

"I thought, seeing as I'm so crippled, you might help me take them off," he murmured.

She slanted him a pixyish grin. "I'm not real good with belt buckles, as you might recall."

"I figured I could handle that part."

"Let's see you do it, then." She planted her hands on her hips and tapped one foot meaningfully. Madam Principal.

Mitch shifted his hips suggestively as he pretended to fumble with the clasp. His leg was hurting again, but he ignored it.

He gave the buckle a couple of halfhearted tugs. "Oh, darn, Miss Bingham. Could you help me?"

She burst out laughing. "You're incorrigible!"

"Is that one of them big-city words?" he teased.

"That's one of them lawyer words!" she returned. "And I ought to sue you for fraud!"

He feigned wide-eyed innocence. "But ma'am, I really can't seem to get it unfastened."

"Oh?" He could have sworn he saw a twinkle in her eye as she undid the rest of her buttons. "Gee, then I guess you can't do anything about *this.*"

Slowly she slipped off her blouse, revealing the round tops of her breasts above a lacy black bra. Mitch's body got hard in what must have been record time.

Now he really *wasn't* sure he could get the belt off without a struggle.

"Or this." She unsnapped her jeans and lowered the zipper slowly, tooth by tooth. Black satin panties peeked at him.

When had his hands gotten damp? Annoyed at himself, Mitch yanked on the buckle in earnest. His action seemed to rouse its stubborn tendencies, and instead of coming loose, the metal prong burrowed tighter into the leather.

"I guess you're what the kids might call NATO—No Action, Talk Only," Kate taunted as she lowered her jeans with a mocking wiggle.

"It's stuck." Mitch couldn't recall when he'd been so frustrated. "I think it's got a mind of its own."

"Your belt?" she challenged. "Or are you referring to something else?"

He wanted to claim he would make her pay for that remark. But threats could only make him look even more ridiculous as he gave the belt another yank and his traitorous hands slipped on the tooled surface.

Reaching behind her to unhook the bra, Kate leaned forward and displayed the inviting valley between her breasts. "I guess I'll just have to put on my swimsuit all by myself, then. You having fun over there?"

Mitch was contemplating grabbing a kitchen knife and slicing through his belt when he felt the prong slip ever so slightly. The darn thing *did* have a mind of its own, he decided in amazement. It must have read his thoughts and decided to yield out of pure self-preservation.

His lips curving in anticipation, he unworked the buckle. It took about thirty milliseconds for the rest of his clothes to hit the floor before he strode across the room and caught Kate still struggling with an errant bra snap.

"Let me help you with that." While her hands were busy behind her back, he lowered her sideways onto the couch and pulled the bra down to bare her breasts.

"Mitch! I'm not finished—"

"Don't let me distract you." Bending over her, he cupped her breasts in his hands and caught them with his lips. Her skin smelled like flowers.

Her breathing quickened and, finished with the bra, she reached for him. Mitch's entire being came to a white-hot point, but he enjoyed the agonizing delay as his mouth met hers and their tongues entwined.

It struck him that Kate had discovered her sexuality with a vengeance. Heaven knew, he was certainly learning new things about his own responsiveness every time they made love.

She released him suddenly and scooted back a few inches. Mitch was about to lean over her when she sat up and, with a twist of pressure on his chest, pushed him down and swung astride.

Her tongue ran down his throat and across his chest, touching each of his nipples and then straying lower. Much as he had enjoyed mastering her, he discovered now that it was even more fun to let her torment and tantalize him.

Mitch couldn't believe a woman so inexperienced could be so daring. She caught him in her mouth and he thought for a moment he might explode.

His heart was pounding so hard Kate must surely have heard it, because she lifted her head to regard him with astonishment. "You're almost ready?" she said.

"What do you mean, almost?" The words tore from his throat.

Delight flashed in her eyes as she mounted him. One hard push sent him soaring almost to heaven.

He had to hold on. He had to make this good for

her, too, but his need was so intense it bordered on painful.

Wriggling against him so her breasts danced across his chest, Kate moved cautiously along his shaft. He couldn't bear it, couldn't wait, had to propel himself into her so hard that she gasped.

Mitch knew he ought to stop, but a primal force greater than his will powered him onward. Kate answered his thrusts with her own, and abruptly he realized that she was crying out with a sheer joyous ache that matched his own.

A golden light pulsed through his body and he let the groans rip from him as his need erupted. Above him, Kate's movements speeded up, and then she shuddered for a long wonderful moment.

She slid down beside him and Mitch held her close.

After a long while, they showered together, found their swimsuits and made their way to the hot tub.

It was secluded among some bushes and, to Mitch's relief, mercifully empty. He was in no mood to make idle conversation with strangers when all he wanted to do was look at Kate.

Across from him, she stretched her arms along the rim and leaned back, luxuriating in the heat. The one-piece suit outlined the soft mounds of her breasts and, in the steam, wisps of hair clung to her cheeks.

Yearning spread through him to see her in a thousand unstudied poses, from the moment she slid out of bed in the morning until she removed her contact lenses at night. He wanted to watch her at the ranch, enjoying a pancake breakfast, giving orders to the hired hands, perhaps nursing an orphaned calf.

And, best of all, returning with him from a horseback ride and adjourning to the barn for a very private riding session in the hayloft.

Once he'd proven his innocence and reclaimed his ranch, he had to find a way to make her stay.

back ride and then turning to the barn for a few typically riling exchanges at the horse.

Once he'd shaven his mustache and medicated his ankle properly, he'd know for sure.

Chapter Eleven

Kate's newfound sense of relaxation, of letting time drift and eddy, sustained her until Monday morning. Then, as the hour to confront Loretta drew near, knife-edged tension replaced it.

Mitch withdrew into his own world. The amber eyes grew opaque; the jaw tightened; and he grimaced whenever he flinched, as if angry at his own body and its residual soreness.

While they stowed everything away in the camper in preparation for a possible rapid departure with Loretta, a stranger once again moved beside Kate. His gaze was far away, and, after he finished sweeping the floor, he went outside without a word.

She didn't object. The truth was, her mind had developed a turmoil of its own.

Something fundamental had changed inside her this weekend. When she and Mitch first made love, Kate realized, she hadn't been emotionally prepared to accept a complete reordering of her plans and dreams.

After yesterday, however, she could no longer fool herself into believing that life would ever go back to the way it had been. She couldn't marry Moose.

She wasn't sure she could marry Mitch, either. But

he had awakened an unsuspected part of her, a tender, passionate woman who wanted a man capable of arousing her.

Outside, Kate could hear him disconnecting the water and electrical hookups. With a sigh, she finished stacking clean dishes in the cabinet and turned to pack her clothes.

Over the past few days, she'd begun keeping her things in a drawer instead of her suitcase. Now it occurred to her that, depending on what happened today, she and Mitch might have to part company quickly, even if, she hoped, temporarily.

Pulling her suitcase from beneath the couch, Kate snapped it open. From the bathroom, she fetched her swimsuit, which had finally dried but still smelled of chlorine.

She held it to her nose, swept by memories of lounging in the hot tub after making love to Mitch. She didn't want to leave Santa Fe, or this trailer park, or this camper. Not ever.

She didn't want to go back to being Kate Bingham of Grazer's Corners, ever-practical, always tightly in control of her emotions. But she wasn't sure who else she could be.

They had to take things one step at a time, she told herself firmly. Until they found Loretta and cleared Mitch of the murder charge, there was no point in speculating about the future.

Forcing herself to focus on the task at hand, Kate tucked the swimsuit into the suitcase and folded a knit top with such meticulous care that not a single wrinkle survived.

As HE ADDED a quart of oil beneath the truck's hood, Mitch's thoughts flashed back to a day nearly twenty years ago when a tornado alert had been issued for the Gulch City area.

He and his father had dropped everything to batten down the hatches. With the help of the ranch hands, they'd brought in the cattle, put the goats and horses in the barn, cooped up the chickens and nailed boards across every window.

With the threat of annihilation hanging over their heads, nothing else had mattered. Mitch's eager antic- ipation of college, his father's concern about paying off the loan, even the worry over his mother's diabe- tes, had momentarily disappeared.

When black clouds blotted the daylight, everyone had retreated into the tornado shelter, a pair of under- ground rooms lined with thick concrete. One of the Hispanic workers had strummed a guitar, leading the others in songs like "The Yellow Rose of Texas" and "Streets of Laredo."

They'd emerged to find only minimal damage, a few ripped fences and some shingles knocked from the roof. After a brief period of jubilation, the every- day joys and cares had returned to center stage.

Preparing the camper for their departure roused in him some of the same feelings of girding against im- pending disaster, and there was no guarantee that the ending would be so fortunate. Anything could happen today, including the possibility that Loretta might have Mitch arrested or that the Tiny Wheeler gang would show up and shoot him. Or that his cousin or Kate might be injured.

Kate. He wanted his mind to linger on the way she'd felt yesterday when he was inside her, and how they'd slept with their arms around each other. But the looming confrontation drove away everything except this day and the events that might unfold.

Shortly after noon, with the camper packed and the truck humming, they arrived outside the adobe headquarters of the Pocket Opera Company. Among the scattering of vehicles, Mitch didn't see his cousin's silver Taurus.

"I'll check inside," Kate said. When he started to come with her, she gestured him back. "Just in case Loretta posted a lookout for you, I'd better go alone."

"If you're not back in five minutes, I'm coming in."

She started to laugh. "Mitch, this isn't a den of desperadoes! We're talking about music auditions here. Do you think somebody's going to knock me unconscious by singing a high *E*-flat?"

"One of the Tiny Wheeler gang could be hiding in there," he grumbled.

"Subtlety isn't exactly their style, in case you hadn't noticed." She jumped down, shut the truck door and went into the building.

Mitch drummed his fingers on the steering wheel and watched the street. He'd parked to one side, closer to the adjacent dentist's office than to the opera building. Nevertheless, Loretta might notice him, so he had to make sure he spotted her before she could flee.

Just when he was starting to get concerned, Kate marched back to the truck. Her forehead puckered as she climbed inside, and at first he thought something must be wrong, but then she said, "No sign of her. Everything looks normal."

"Was the singing that bad?"

"What?"

"You're frowning."

"Oh. No, that's not the problem." She sank back in her seat, blond hair spilling across the worn upholstery. "They're doing *Così Fan Tutte*." She said the title of the opera as if it ought to mean something to him.

Mitch searched his memory. His grandmother had sometimes played a recording of the Mozart work, but all he recalled were some pretty melodies. "Sorry, I don't see the problem."

"It's about these two men who make a bet that their fiancées will be loyal, no matter what," Kate said. "The men pretend to go off to battle, then return in disguise and court each others' girlfriends."

"So?" Mitch said.

"And the women fall for them! They're so fickle! Am I like that? Do you think I'm fickle because I left my groom on my wedding day and got involved with another man?"

"I hadn't thought about it, and frankly, I don't care." It was the most honest answer Mitch could give.

She stared gloomily out the windshield. "It's depressing! For two hundred years, people have been poking fun at those two disloyal women. What would they say about me?"

"Look at it this way," Mitch said. "There are worse fates than being immortalized."

"Nobody else in Grazer's Corners has ever run off on their wedding day," Kate continued as if she hadn't heard. "You won't catch Jordan Grazer pulling a stunt like that. Or Hailey Olson, either."

"Who are Jordan Grazer and Hailey Olson?"

"The other June brides." Kate sank deeper into her seat. "Look at the legacy I left them—a bunch of bullet holes in the church walls. I always thought the townspeople would remember me as a shining example of something-or-other. They sure will, but that something-or-other isn't mentionable in polite company."

Mitch wasn't sure whether to chuckle or put his arm around her. He did neither, because at that moment his gaze fixed on a silver Taurus tooling along the street toward them.

"That's her," he said even though he couldn't yet make out the driver's face or the license number.

"How can you be sure?"

"Her car pulls to the right." He shook his head. "How can she drive across the country like that?"

"She should have asked you to fix it."

"She should have asked me to fix a lot of things." He studied the other vehicles on the street, but there was no sign of the rusty van. Maybe luck was with them and Tiny Wheeler and crew had gotten sidetracked.

The Taurus turned into the lot and parked in front of the building. The driver's door opened and a slender, stocking-clad leg descended.

"I don't see how people do that," Kate muttered as they waited for the rest of Loretta to emerge.

"Do what?"

"She's wearing a gold chain around her ankle. I tried that once and it snagged my stocking."

"Kate," he said, "what's wrong with my cousin? Why isn't she getting out?"

He heard a tongue click beside him. "Obviously, she's collecting her stuff."

Sure enough, a moment later Loretta stepped out, a large purse hooked over her shoulder and a sheaf of sheet music beneath one arm. She swung around to lock the car.

"Now?" Kate said.

"Now."

They jumped down and crossed the lot with long strides. By the time Loretta had finished fumbling with the lock and picking up the sheet music she managed to drop in the process, the two of them came abreast of her.

"What... Oh, my God!" Wide olive-colored eyes stared at Mitch. He glimpsed a trace of the hero worship that had been her customary expression as a child, and then her expression hardened. "How dare you! This is my life, and I want you to stay out of it!"

"Loretta?" said Kate. "Do you remember me?"

Tossing back her curly brown hair, Loretta swung around. She blinked, and then recognition dawned. "Miss Bingham! What are you doing here?"

"Your friend Horst said I inspired you to go back to the ranch." Mitch knew Kate well enough to realize she was struggling to find the best words to get through to his cousin. "So I felt responsible when I found out you might be in danger."

Loretta tightened her grip on her music. "The only dangerous person around here is Mitch! He's a wanted criminal, did you know that?"

Kate nodded. "I'm the sheriff in Grazer's Corners now. I'm well aware of his status."

The younger girl's mouth twisted in disbelief. "You're the sheriff, and you're helping him?"

"The Tiny Wheeler gang knows you're in Santa Fe." Kate spoke gently but firmly. "We think they want to eliminate you as a witness."

A tiny gulp betrayed Loretta's reaction, but she

braced herself, feet apart. "Look, Miss Bingham, I appreciated your help in raising my scholarship, but my life isn't your problem. I can take care of myself."

The girl might be twenty-five, but she hadn't matured much. "For Pete's sake, use a little common sense!" Mitch blurted. "You can't deal with a bunch of armed men!"

She refused even to look at him. "Excuse me, Miss Bingham. I've got an audition scheduled." With that, Loretta wheeled and marched into the building.

Mitch would have followed, but Kate put a warning hand on his arm. "We'll make things worse if we intrude. Besides, we need to keep a lookout for the van."

Reluctantly, he yielded. But what if Loretta slipped out a back door?

"I've got an idea. Come this way." Catching Kate's elbow, he guided her to the side of the building, where potted trees shaded a bench. "You can sit here in comfort and watch the front without anyone noticing."

"What are you going to do?"

"A little alley skulking," Mitch replied. "Can you whistle loud?"

"You're talking to a school principal here." Putting two fingers in her mouth, she let out a blast so sharp it made him jump.

"Thank you for waking up the entire neighborhood," Mitch said dryly. "I guess I'll be able to hear that."

"One whistle if it's Loretta, two if it's those maniacs," Kate said.

"Three if you want the sonic boom to level the entire city," he couldn't resist adding as they parted.

The alley was a service lane that ran the length of

the block. On the far side, it was edged by two post-age-stamp backyards, one nearly overgrown with trees, the other crammed with a swing set and ride-on toys. From one of the small houses, he heard the clatter of pots and pans and a woman calling to her children.

The opera building had a smooth-walled back, except for a single door, which stood open. Mitch moved as close to it as he dared, then lounged against the wall.

From inside, he heard a man speaking. A piano began the familiar chords of a Mozart aria.

Mitch hadn't heard his cousin sing in more than a decade, but he recognized her voice instantly. It sounded like Grandma's, the same round, sweet tone and effortless high notes, only younger and fuller.

He remembered enough Italian from his childhood to recognize that she was singing about remaining as immovable and steadfast as a rock. But it wasn't the words that mattered, it was the music.

A shiver ran through him at her pure clarity, and he realized he was also reacting to the heartfelt emotion of the song. All the openness and yearning that Loretta refused to display in real life, she channeled into her art.

When singing was so obviously what she loved, why had she put it aside to go back to the ranch? Why had she stooped to taking a job as Billy Parkinson's secretary?

In some way, Mitch suspected, whatever she was seeking must be tied up with the music that ran through Loretta's veins. But what was it?

The final notes of the aria drifted into the afternoon

air like a breath of perfume. He hardly dared swallow until it ended.

The man began talking again. Mitch caught the words *already cast* and *perhaps later* and *Musetta*.

He recognized the name of a character from the opera *La Bohème*. Apparently his cousin had missed her chance with the first production but might have a shot at a later one.

Just in case Loretta decided to exit this way, he waited until he heard a sharp whistle from Kate. It came only once.

He strode around the building in time to see the two women facing each other next to Loretta's car. As he approached, he heard Kate saying, "They laid an ambush for us in Arizona. We were nearly killed."

Disbelief and scorn flashed from Loretta's eyes. "You mean you drove out here with Mitch? Just the two of you? You're involved with him, aren't you, Miss Bingham?"

He half wished Kate would lie to preserve her credibility. But he knew she was incapable of it.

"Not at first, but it turned out that way," he heard her say. "That doesn't change anything."

"It makes you a little less than objective!" snapped Loretta. "Let me give *you* a warning, Miss Bingham. Mitch doesn't care about anyone but himself."

He came closer. "Loretta, I wish I'd explained things to you earlier."

She flinched at the sound of his voice, and for an instant he saw vulnerability and embarrassment on her face. Then the icy facade returned, like a mask. "You wish you'd explained things, or that you'd given me excuses I might have swallowed?"

"Loretta, I *was* trying to save the ranch."

"Oh, sure!" Her lip curled in distaste. "Then why did you spend the money on law school instead of paying off the loan?"

"Billy had already foreclosed," he said. "I tried to arrange payments but he refused."

"Besides, this isn't about the ranch anymore," Kate added. "Mitch is facing a murder charge and he needs you to testify that he fired in self-defense."

"He's a lawyer," Loretta snarled. "He can get himself off! Besides, if he hadn't shown up, I was right on the brink of..." She caught herself. "...of nothing!"

Her eyes brimming with unshed tears, she wrenched open the car door. Then she shot them a defiant glare.

"There's no point in you following me, because I won't help you!" she said. "I'm just going to pick up a few things I left at a motel room—the other people there, they're musicians, kind of free spirits, so don't try to involve them."

"Friends of yours?" Kate asked.

Loretta shrugged. "I invited them to a party, and they stayed. It got kind of crowded for me, so after the first night, I decided to hang out at Sally's place."

"They're not living off you, are they?" Mitch demanded.

His cousin glared. "I'm not stupid. I just paid for one night and then they made their own arrangement with the manager. Anyway, the opera's already cast, so I'm leaving. If you come after me, I swear, I'll call the police!"

She jumped inside, slammed the door and took off without fastening her seat belt. Kate look as if she wanted to call out a reminder, but thought the better of it.

Mitch watched in dismay as his only hope of proving his innocence vanished down the street. After such a long journey and so many close calls, he felt frozen in place by disappointment.

Kate grabbed his arm. "What are you waiting for?" she demanded. "After her!"

He was about to remind Kate that chasing his cousin would only get him arrested, when something occurred to him. If Loretta had charged her night at the motel on her credit card, Billy Parkinson might have tracked her down. If so, and if she were now headed to the motel to visit her friends, she would have a reception committee waiting for her.

He broke into a run toward the truck. Kate pelted after him.

As THEY ROLLED down the street in the wake of the Taurus, Kate was surprised and not entirely pleased to find herself reacting to Loretta's stubbornness with relief.

If his cousin had agreed to vouch for him, Mitch wouldn't need Kate's help anymore. Their odyssey would end, either with her return, alone, to Grazer's Corners, or—

Or what? She hadn't figured that out yet, and she was glad to have the day of reckoning postponed.

On the other hand, she *wasn't* glad that Loretta might be walking into a trap, as Mitch had just pointed out. And she certainly wasn't glad that the man she loved still faced a murder charge.

"Which way?" he asked as they came to an intersection.

Straight ahead, a traffic jam blocked the road, and there was no sign of the silver car in either direction.

Kate had the impression—so fleeting it might almost have been a momentary blurring of her contact lens—that she'd glimpsed a vehicle turning right, and said so.

Sure enough, a block later they caught sight of the Taurus whipping around another corner. The height of the truck's cab gave them an advantage as they struggled to keep it in sight without attracting attention.

"I don't understand why she won't listen to reason," Mitch growled as he drove.

"I do." Kate had seen the same attitude in angry teenagers one summer when she'd taught high school remedial classes. "She has a mental image of herself as a helpless kid and you as an all-powerful adult. She thinks you can control everything that happens."

"Don't I wish?" The Stetson cast a shadow over his face but she could hear the frustration in his words.

They rounded another bend and Kate spotted the silver car entering a motel parking lot. Mitch slowed the truck as they cruised by.

"I don't see Tiny's van," he said.

"Those bandits aren't *that* stupid," Kate suggested, although she wasn't entirely convinced of that. "If they're here, they've had plenty of time to hide it."

Mitch pulled to the curb and they watched his cousin hop out of her car. Key in hand, Loretta walked toward Room 104.

In the room's window, something glinted where the curtains had been pushed aside. Kate blinked and focused harder. She hadn't been mistaken; sunlight was reflecting off the muzzle of a gun.

"They're inside!" she cried, but her voice didn't carry to Loretta.

Nothing mattered to Kate at that moment except the

fact that a young girl, a student whom she herself had influenced, was walking into a death trap. Without hesitation, she wrenched open her door, jumped down and barreled across the sidewalk and the asphalt, yelling, "Wait! Wait! Wait!"

Loretta turned with a frown. Kate pelted toward her, her heart and lungs threatening to burst from a combination of adrenaline and speed.

Behind her, she heard the truck roar into gear and knew Mitch must be hurrying toward the entrance to the parking lot. If only that weren't half a block away!

Loretta stood frozen on the sidewalk. Kate was still a dozen feet from her when the door to Room 104 banged open and all three bandits tried to rush through it at the same time.

Stuck in the middle, the tall skinny one, Dexter Dinkens, let out a string of curses that turned the air blue. Wedged behind him, the massive Tiny Wheeler gave a shove that sent Dexter stumbling onto the sandaled, sock-clad foot of Nine Toes Blankenship, who let out a scream so high-pitched and unearthly it would surely have won him a role of some sort from the opera company, if only for its novelty value.

In that brief window of time before the bandits could disentangle themselves, Kate grabbed the younger woman and pulled her toward her car.

The Taurus was unlocked, thank goodness. Kate pushed Loretta into the driver's seat.

From the far side of Room 104, the truck jounced toward them. It loomed, massive and unmistakable, in the cramped lot, and with horror Kate saw Dexter Dinkins raise his shotgun and take aim at Mitch.

She jumped into the car beside Loretta. "Honk your

horn! Distract him!'' When the girl didn't move fast enough, Kate reached over and pushed it herself.

The blare nearly deafened her. "You'll get us killed!'' Loretta cried, finally coming to life. She quickly turned the key in the ignition.

They backed out, fast. Dexter took aim again at Mitch, only to be jostled as Tiny Wheeler thrust past, racing toward the Taurus. Her panic yielding to fury, Loretta floored it and zoomed past the truck toward the exit.

Mitch! He couldn't turn around in this cramped space, but Nine Toes Blankenship, who appeared to care less about the man who was escaping than about the man who had stepped on his foot, began pummeling Dexter's shoulder. Tiny turned to yell at them both, and the truck lumbered past, still headed in the opposite direction from the Taurus.

"He'll have to come out a different way!" Kate said. "Circle around and we'll meet him..."

A police car turned onto the block. For one heart-stopping moment, she thought someone had reported Mitch. Then she realized it was cruising toward the three bandits, who stood in front of the motel trying without much success to hide their shotguns.

Swiveling, Kate saw Mitch's truck disappear down a side street. Of course he wouldn't hang around, not with an All Points Bulletin issued. Besides, if the police weren't already hunting him, Tiny Wheeler would put them on the scent.

"Just tell me where you want me to drop you," Loretta said tightly as they distanced themselves from the motel. Mitch was out of sight.

If only the two of them had arranged a meeting place in case they got separated! But the possibility hadn't occurred to them. Now, with growing dismay, Kate realized that there was no easy way to contact him. She wondered what had happened to Loretta's friends, but Loretta assured her they'd probably had auditions of their own.

Kate concentrated her concern on Mitch. He couldn't be more than a mile away. But he might as well be in another city or state for all the likelihood of finding him.

She couldn't give up so easily. "Try that direction." She pointed toward where she'd last seen the truck. "We need to intercept him. Maybe he's pulled over to wait for us."

Loretta shrugged. "If you say so."

They drove around for half an hour. Traffic was heavy, but even so, Kate felt sure they would have spotted the truck had Mitch been watching for them.

Obviously he had decided it was unsafe to linger in the area. Surely he would try to meet her somewhere, but where?

Not the central plaza; he was too likely to attract attention there. Maybe the RV park.

Grudgingly, Loretta swung by the location. But there was no sign of Mitch outside it, and, inside, their slot had already been taken by a new arrival.

They tried the music store and the opera company headquarters. No sign of him.

Loretta was clearly impatient, and Kate didn't blame her. It was time to accept the painful truth.

She had lost Mitch.

No goodbyes, no chance to try to work things out, nothing. He was gone and, for his own safety, she could only hope he wouldn't stick around Santa Fe.

It was time to return to Grazer's Corners. Time to

face Moose and the townspeople, and a life that had just had a great hole blasted through it.

Someday, if she were lucky, she might hear from Mitch again. Certainly, as sheriff, she could keep tabs on the status of Gulch City's investigation. But...

But she wanted him *now*. She missed his quiet strength, the sudden sunshine of his smile, the aroma of cedar and masculinity.

She missed the slight roughness of his cheek against hers, and the gentleness of his mouth, and the way he angled himself over her when they made love. She wanted to wake up and see Mitch standing at the stove making coffee, with the morning light playing across the planes of his face.

But she couldn't.

"I guess it's time for me to go back to California," she said.

"Bus station okay?" Loretta asked. "Or I can take you to the airport."

On the point of replying, Kate realized she hadn't thought this matter through. "What are you going to do, after I leave?"

Loretta pressed her lips together and didn't answer for a minute. Finally she parked in front of a convenience store.

"I suppose it's safe to tell you, since you won't be seeing Mitch," she replied. "I'm going to the High C."

"The ranch?" Instead of answering, Loretta got out of the car and marched toward the store. Kate followed, perplexed. "Why? And what are you doing here?"

"Laying in supplies." Inside the store, Loretta grabbed a wire basket and began piling it with toiletry items. "After what happened at the motel, I don't dare go back to Sally's house. I'm heading straight for Texas."

Impulsively, Kate picked up a basket, too. She'd left all her supplies with Mitch except for what was in her purse, which, fortunately, included her glasses, her credit cards and her birth control pills. But not much else.

At the same time, she had to talk sense into Loretta. "You can't go back there," she said as she tossed a package of contact lens cleaner into her basket. "You saw what those men are like."

"They're mostly bluff," Loretta told her. "Billy Parkinson would never hurt me. Anyway, I know when it's safe to go to the ranch. On Sunday mornings, everybody goes to church—it's one of Billy's rules. I'll be fine, Miss Bingham."

"Can you tell me what you're searching for?"

A headshake set the mass of brown curls bouncing. "Sorry. That's my secret."

Loretta didn't have an ounce of sense, Kate thought. She'd nearly walked straight into Tiny Wheeler's arms—or the sights of his gun—a few minutes ago, and here she was determined to march into the lions' den.

Someone needed to keep an eye on her. And as she regarded her nearly full basket, Kate realized she'd already made a decision.

"Mind if I come with you?" she asked.

Something that might have been relief shone in Loretta's eyes. "I guess it couldn't hurt," she said. "I don't much like driving alone."

As they paid at the register and departed, it occurred

to Kate that this way she might see Mitch again, after all.

It would be safer for him if he didn't figure out their destination and come after them. But for Loretta's and her own safety, and for the sake of the throbbing ache inside her chest, she hoped he would.

Chapter Twelve

Mitch had always known that someday he was likely to lose Kate. But he hadn't been prepared for it to happen yet.

Damn it, he thought as he cruised along Paseo Peralta, he didn't want to lose her, ever. Crazy as it seemed, given his present circumstances and the fact that she had no desire to spend the rest of her life on a ranch, he intended to marry that woman.

First, though, he had to find her. And that wasn't going to happen in Santa Fe.

He'd driven by the music store, the opera headquarters and the plaza, but there'd been no sign of Kate. He'd approached the RV park only to see a police car turning in at the gate. It might be a coincidence, but maybe not, since he'd had to register his license number with the office.

So Kate was gone, although, presumably, safe. She would probably return to Grazer's Corners.

That was exactly where Mitch would go, too.

Even though he had nothing to offer Kate now, he couldn't let her marry Moose. The man was wrong for her.

In his mind, an image of Kate took shape, not a flat

photographic picture but the warm rosy reality of her. Glowing skin, swingy blond hair, bright blue eyes.

He could see her slender figure planting itself in front of the trading post, defying the show-off biker. And hear her earsplitting whistle alerting him that Loretta had emerged from the audition.

No wonder he could hear her. His ears were still ringing.

There couldn't possibly be another woman in the world like Kate. Mitch refused to give her up, even though from this angle the future resembled a patch of quicksand more than a sea of opportunity.

He wasn't looking forward to making the long drive back through Arizona. Neither would Kate, he supposed. She would probably catch a plane rather than a bus.

The airport lay in the same general direction as the freeway. He decided to swing by there on his way out of town, just in case he could spot her.

ON CERRILLOS ROAD, Mitch went right by the office with its cactus-shaped shingle reading J. C. Lopez-Gaucho M.D., General Podiatry before he realized what he had seen.

A rusty van with Texas plates sat wedged between a Mercedes and a Volvo in front of the building. The Tiny Wheeler gang had been released.

At the motel, Nine Toes Blankenship had been hopping around on an obviously injured foot. He must have stopped to get it checked. Then, with Billy no doubt tracking Loretta by her credit charges, they'd be hot on her trail.

Mitch's gut twisted with anger. For the past ten

years, his every attempt to set the world right had backfired.

When he'd finally gone to the ranch to try to reach an agreement with Billy, he'd barely escaped with his life. Since then, at least, he'd had a clear-cut goal: to find his cousin and prove his innocence.

Instead, he had put Loretta's and Kate's lives in jeopardy. Going to Grazer's Corners might satisfy his emotional need to see Kate, but it would leave his cousin unprotected.

As long as he was on the lam, he couldn't even track Loretta. It was time to stop running around like a crazed coyote and start thinking about what was best for the people he loved.

Grimly, Mitch pulled into a service station and set to filling his tank. He would be hitting the freeway, all right, but he wouldn't be traveling to California.

It was time he went back to Gulch City and turned himself in.

LATE ON SATURDAY, Kate and Loretta came within fifteen miles of Gulch City. They didn't want to risk being recognized, so they stayed at a bed-and-breakfast in nearby Fort Jenkins.

It had taken them five days to make what should have been at most a three-day drive from Santa Fe. That was because they'd had to spend two nights in El Paso after a tire blew.

Kate remembered what Mitch had said about the Taurus pulling to the right. Well, the pulling had finally worn through one of the tires.

Fortunately, it happened at a traffic light, so all they suffered was a little jostling. Also the embarrassment of having to wait for a tow truck while horns honked and motorists glared.

Then it turned out that Loretta's car had some kind of front-end problem which required ordering parts. The two of them used the time to run laundry and do a little shopping.

Kate found her companion warm, impulsive and determined. She hadn't, however, learned what it was that the young woman expected to find on the ranch. In fact, Loretta didn't like talking about any aspect of the months she'd spent working for Billy.

Kate's explanation of how Mitch really lost the ranch was met with apparent indifference. Loretta also refused to acknowledge that only her testimony could save Mitch from a murder charge. In her view, her clever, capable cousin should simply use his legal training to extricate himself.

When Kate pressed the issue, Loretta put a tape on her cassette player and sang. It was frustrating, but heavenly.

Now they had negotiated their way into the heart of Texas, through rolling grasslands and fenced ranches bearing names like the Flying KW and Split Lightning. What buildings Kate could see from the highway were weathered and rambling.

On their way into Fort Jenkins, they rolled past the stone schoolhouse where a custodian was checking the playground equipment, no doubt planning to make good use of the summer break. Kate got an achy feeling when she thought of Grazer's Corners Elementary and was surprised to realize she missed the place already.

A cheery lady rented them two rooms at the bed-and-breakfast. Kate put the charge on her card, since she assumed Billy Parkinson would be tracking any purchases Loretta made.

For dinner, they ate sandwiches in Kate's room. They didn't dare go out for fear someone would recognize Loretta and report her to Billy.

Push had come to shove, Kate reflected. Tomorrow, unless she could talk Loretta out of it, they were going to sneak onto the ranch. A ranch where they might find themselves up against some very unethical men.

At the prospect of staring down the barrel of a gun, Kate's hands went cold and her feet got prickly. Her tongue felt thick, too. She hoped she wouldn't react this way if she got cornered and needed her wits about her.

Sitting on the carpet, Loretta propped herself against the edge of the bed. "The church service starts at ten. Billy makes all his hands go with him."

"He's religious?" The notion didn't gibe with Kate's impression of the man.

"No way," said Loretta. "He just likes to look good to the town's wheelers and dealers."

"Like Chief Novo."

"Yeah, and the mayor and the country club set. You know how snobby small towns can be."

Kate thought of Grazer's Corners. "Yes. But sometimes the movers and shakers are simply the people willing to take responsibility for getting things done."

"I suppose," Loretta conceded. "Anyway, there's some Hispanic families that live on the ranch, too. One of the men, Mario, was Uncle Carl's foreman, and Billy kept him on. Those families drive about twenty miles to a Catholic church, so they're gone all morning, too."

"Billy doesn't leave anyone on the property for

safekeeping?'' Kate asked dubiously. ''What if there was a fire?''

''It's only empty for a couple of hours,'' Loretta said. ''Besides, this isn't California. People leave their doors unlocked.''

''Is that how we're going to get into the house?''

''We don't need to,'' replied the younger woman. ''We won't be going inside.''

''No? Then where...'' Kate caught a warning gleam in Loretta's eyes. No use asking; she wouldn't get an answer. ''What if we get caught?'' she asked instead.

''I told you, Billy won't hurt me,'' Loretta said easily. ''He hates Mitch—he always has. Some kind of male testosterone thing. He's too smart to kill somebody in cold blood, anyway, and his clowns are probably still tripping and staggering around the Santa Fe jail.''

Kate wished she could be sure of that, but she didn't intend to play it safe now. If she hadn't trusted her instincts these past few weeks, she'd still be in Grazer's Corners, and married to Moose. *That* would have been a terrible mistake.

She only hoped that breaking into the High C ranch tomorrow wouldn't prove an even worse one.

MITCH CAMPED Saturday night in a grove of trees on the Bar L ranch twenty miles from town and several miles from the ranch house. To be on the safe side, he ate a cold meal and restrained his impulse to go for a walk. He was in no hurry to get himself arrested, even though he had come all this distance for that very purpose.

He kept wondering where Kate was, and hoping she'd had the good sense to call off her wedding.

In spite of everything, he dreamed of a future in which he regained the High C and took back his place in society. A future in which he and Kate got married and settled down, as Gulch City families had been doing for more than a century.

Kate would like the area once she came to know it, he thought, stretching out along the bed. She would enjoy the potluck socials at the ranches, and square dancing at the country club, and the homemade floats at the town's Fourth of July parade.

He could smell her floral freshness on the sheets. Something essential about her pervaded the camper. For the chance of holding her in his arms again, Mitch would risk almost anything.

Except, he realized with a pang, that he had very little left to risk. Here he was, within a few miles of the place where he'd been born, forced to skulk like an intruder.

Outside the camper, a twig cracked. Mitch's heart slammed into overdrive and he leaped to his feet, only to find himself staring out the window into the broad, placid face of a cow. It regarded him with wide-set dark eyes, then lowered its head and ambled off.

His blood still thundered and his muscles were tight. Damn, he was jumpy, just when he'd thought himself resigned to his fate.

Slowly Mitch realized what was bothering him. He was about to place his life in the hands of Norris Novo, and he didn't trust the man.

He visualized the chief: a broad, impassive face and a mouth with an impatient twitch. Novo was loyal to his buddies, skeptical of anything he couldn't see or touch, and had little regard for the finer points of the law.

Not that Mitch held a grudge against the town's top cop. Although it was Novo who'd evicted him from his ranch, it had been done in a courteous manner. And he couldn't blame the chief for wanting to arrest him in the shooting of Jules Kominsky.

But the ambush in Oak Creek Canyon was another matter. What if the chief had been directly involved? If so, once Mitch was in custody, he might not live to stand trial.

He lowered himself onto the couch, his jaw clenched. He could not, would not turn back from his intention of submitting to arrest.

Until this case was resolved, Loretta remained in danger. And he couldn't even begin to work things out with Kate.

But neither did he have any intention of laying his neck on a chopping block. He had to fix it so Novo couldn't pull anything underhanded.

Mitch might not trust the chief, but he still believed in the people of Gulch City. He'd known most of them all his life.

He would turn himself in at the church tomorrow morning, in front of several hundred of his fellow citizens. He would let them know that if any harm came to him in custody, it was Chief Novo's doing.

That might restrain the man. At least, Mitch hoped so.

He was going to have to stake his life on it.

KATE AWOKE EARLY on Sunday morning. She took her time showering, knowing breakfast wouldn't be served downstairs until eight o'clock.

To her surprise, Loretta arrived at her room at

seven-thirty, dressed in jeans and a T-shirt. Until now, she'd always slept as late as possible.

Plopping into a chair, Loretta began ticking off points on her fingers. "Down at the barn, the hands will be milking and collecting eggs. Somebody'll need to turn the cows and calves out to pasture, and they'll check the weather report in case of twisters. So I don't expect everybody to clear out until half past nine."

Kate listened, impressed. "You really know the routine."

Loretta shrugged. "I love the ranch," she said. "I don't think Mitch ever understood how much."

"Is that what you're looking for?" Kate asked. "Something that proves you're entitled to it?"

The younger woman shook her head. "No. It's something personal. Something worth a lot of money, but I wouldn't sell it. Grandma meant for me to have it."

"You still don't trust me?" Kate asked.

Loretta smiled ruefully. "It's not that. I've got kind of a fetish about it. I think it's bad luck to say anything until it's actually in my hands. At this point, would it make any difference in whether you come with me or not?"

"No," Kate had to admit.

"Then let's go eat breakfast."

At nine-thirty, they drove to a pay phone and Loretta telephoned the ranch. A machine answered and she hung up.

"Looks like they've left," she said as she got back in the car.

Without thinking, Kate blurted, "I wish Mitch were here."

"You love him, don't you?" Loretta started the engine.

"I guess it's hard for you to understand."

"Not really. I had a crush on my cousin for years." They pulled away from the curb and jounced along a two-lane highway. The land was flat and cactus-strewn, although spring rains had turned everything green.

Kate noticed some oil wells punctuating the range, along with a number of fire-ant mounds. She shuddered, grateful that nothing worse than snails and aphids plagued her garden back home.

A pickup passed them, heading toward Gulch City. Loretta averted her face, but it occurred to Kate that someone might recognize the car.

She just hoped Loretta really did know where to look. The less time they spent on the ranch, the better.

DRIVING INTO GULCH CITY was like traveling backward through time.

Mitch turned onto Main Street, and passed the courthouse where he had argued cases and filed wills and divorce papers. His parents' marriage license had been registered there, and his own birth certificate.

A block down City Center Lane lay the Gulch City Free Church, built with squared-off stones as most of the town's early buildings.

Mitch had always assumed that someday, like his father and grandfather, he would stand at the altar in this old stone church. And he knew now that the only woman he wanted to see gliding down the aisle was Kate, her blue eyes luminous and a circlet of roses crowning her blond hair.

But that day, if it ever came, would be a long time off.

Mitch parked and strode along the sidewalk, his boots clicking. A young couple, approaching from the opposite direction, halted and stared at him, open-mouthed.

His back stiffly erect, Mitch turned at the walkway. Out here, the sun shone on a lilac bush and a lush patch of lawn, making the colors glow like stained glass. From inside, he heard an organ playing the introductory notes of a hymn.

Mitch straightened his Stetson. Then he pushed the door wide and entered the shadowed darkness.

A WEATHERED SIGN over the entrance gate read High C Ranch. Loretta stopped in front of the gate. "You'll have to hold it open for me."

"Isn't it locked?"

She shook her head. "There's half a dozen back ways into the ranch, and besides, these fences couldn't keep out anything less clumsy than a steer. Just don't catch your foot in the cattle grate, city slicker."

Kate wasn't about to ask what a cattle grate was. She hurried to the gate and lifted the crossbar, then swung it out while the Taurus rattled across.

The grate, she saw, was exactly what its name implied, a metal grille beneath her feet, covering a slight depression. Kate supposed it must discourage cattle from exiting if the latch came open.

She stepped gingerly across, lifted the crossbar into place and got back in the car. They were now officially trespassing, she realized.

They bumped along the dirt road and around a cluster of trees. Loretta halted in a parking bay beside a scraggly lawn.

A suburban-style ranch house, its white paint peeling and its roof missing some shingles, sat halfway up a slope. Judging by the graceful bay window and latticed porch, someone had once lavished a lot of love on it. Unlike its current occupant.

This place belonged to Mitch, no matter what the law said. Kate had heard the longing in his voice whenever he spoke of home. It was the same deep-down sense of rightness that she felt on the first day of school when she stood out front, welcoming the children.

Past the house, she glimpsed a barn and a corral. "You can't see the storage yard from here," Loretta noted. "Billy's been stocking building materials and hardware to sell to other ranchers. I don't think the operation's paying off as well as he expected, maybe because he cheats people."

"What now?" Kate asked.

"We ring the doorbell," Loretta answered. "No sense in sneaking around until we're sure nobody's home."

As the younger woman marched along a walkway to the front door, Kate lingered behind, gazing across a vista of bush-studded grazing land. She pictured Mitch riding the range, the Stetson shading his face, his knees gripping the saddle.

In the evenings, he would come home to a loving wife who would turn the evening bath into a sensual game for two. A woman who knew exactly what to do with a cowboy's slim hips and muscular thighs...

"No answer." Loretta dusted her hands as she returned. "Let's go make sure nobody's hanging around outside."

At the barn, the smell of cow manure mingled with the pungency of rotting hay. Loretta frowned. "They need to turn that more often. It's going bad."

"I'll bet Mitch didn't let things go," Kate said.

"He sure didn't." She halted, frowning. "Gee, I just thought of something. When Mitch inherited the place, he was the same age I am now. I always pictured him as, well, older. In control of things."

"To a fifteen-year-old, he probably seemed that way." Kate hoped Loretta was finally beginning to realize she'd been unfair to her cousin. If so, the younger woman gave no sign of it.

Seeing no one about, they retreated behind the house to a weed-filled lawn.

"There!" Loretta pointed toward an excavation, where a flight of stone steps descended to a thick door.

"Wine cellar?" Kate asked.

"Tornado shelter." With a glance around, Loretta produced a key. "This is the place we need to search. Coming?"

Kate Bingham had spent almost her entire thirty-one years as a living, breathing Little Miss Goody Two-shoes. In the past two weeks, she had abandoned her groom at the altar, run off with a fugitive, survived several shoot-outs and made love to a man who was not her husband.

She was about to add breaking and entering to that list. It was not a reassuring thought.

"Coming," she said.

Chapter Thirteen

Cold air issued from the cellar as Loretta opened the door. Kate could feel the dankness seeping out into the heat of the day.

"Did you ever use this to escape a tornado?" she asked.

"Not while I was on the ranch." Loretta pushed the door inward. Kate wondered if it wouldn't have been simpler to use a trapdoor flush with the ground, then realized it could get blocked by debris. Whoever built this shelter had designed it with care. Mitch's father, she guessed.

It took a minute or two for Loretta to locate the light switch. When the thin illumination came on, Kate saw that they stood in a small room piled with boxes and furniture. Another room, partially visible through an opening, was similarly cluttered.

"They couldn't get many people in here if a tornado hit, not with all this stuff piled up," Kate said. "It doesn't seem safe."

The younger woman surveyed the room, hands on hips. "Billy tends to do whatever's convenient at the moment and worry about the consequences later. He wanted the regular basement to store building supplies, so he moved the family's old things out here.''

Kate's uneasiness intensified. ''You mean you don't really know if it's here, this thing you're looking for?''

''It has to be.'' Loretta sneezed as she poked at a dusty trunk. ''It isn't anywhere else.''

''You searched the whole house?''

''Yes, bit by bit. That's why I stayed here for so long. Help me move this, would you?'' Loretta indicated the trunk, which was wedged so tightly in place that it couldn't be opened.

They shoved it into the clear, both women straining. When they looked inside, there was nothing but tack equipment.

At least their eyes were adjusting to the dimness. Next time she did this, Kate told herself with irony, she would make certain to bring a flashlight.

As they combed through the boxes, Loretta explained that after she came to work at the ranch, she'd expected to find what she sought without trouble. But she got the sense that she was being watched.

''Or maybe it was just Billy sniffing around me,'' Loretta admitted as she brushed a wisp of hair from her temple. ''He let me know he was interested. I think that's why he hired me. That, and because it let him rub salt into Mitch's wounds.''

''He didn't pressure you to...get involved with him?''

The younger woman shook her head. ''I told him I'd had my heart broken at music school and wasn't ready for a new relationship. He was a real gentleman about it. You see, you can't always believe Mitch. He wouldn't give Billy credit for anything.''

''Did you live at the ranch?''

"I had to," Loretta said. "How else would I get a chance to poke around?"

The woman had been playing with fire. Surely Billy must have been suspicious. Or up to something.

Was he up to something now? Kate went outside and gazed around, but saw nothing amiss.

They finished going through the front room and moved to the back. Aside from a small bathroom, those composed the entire shelter; there wasn't even a kitchen, although one shelf held canned food.

In the back room, someone had wedged in a filing cabinet, more boxes and a large steamer trunk. The women set to work.

Trying to ignore her sore muscles, Kate asked, "What made you decide to return this year instead of earlier?"

"I got my degree midyear." Loretta dug through some old clothes. "I was entering singing contests, going to auditions, but I couldn't seem to focus on my career. Everything reminded me of Grandma Luisa. I decided it was time to take care of unfinished business."

"Are you ever going to tell me what we're looking for?" she asked. "I might see it and not recognize it."

Loretta gave her a crooked smile. "Don't worry. It won't get by us."

Kate checked her watch. It was nearly eleven. If the church service began at ten, it might be ending. "We ought to go."

"Not yet!" Loretta struggled with a latch on the steamer trunk, which, on end, stood about four feet high. "I'd just managed to swipe the key and get it duplicated, and then Mitch came stomping in and shot Jules. I let myself get scared off, but not this time.

There!'' She pried the first latch open and started on the second.

A scritching noise reached Kate. It might have been a mouse scurrying beneath the boxes, or a loose piece of gravel rattling down the outside stairs. "I'd better go check..."

"Hold that!" Loretta indicated a strap on the outside of the trunk. "Now pull!"

Kate followed Loretta's instructions. Straining and grunting, they slowly pulled the steamer open.

Stale perfume wafted out. Inside, glittery dresses and a velvet cape hung from a bar, while drawers lined the other side.

Loretta appeared to be holding her breath as she opened one of drawer. It was full of sheet music.

The younger woman's eyes widened, and then she grimaced. "Oh, no."

"What's wrong?"

"It's printed music. I mean, some of it could be interesting, but..." She slid open a second drawer and a third, and let out a long, disappointed breath. "More of the same."

"And what we're looking for would be—?" Kate let the question dangle.

"Handwritten," Loretta said. "And very old."

Music. They must be looking for an original music manuscript. "Who wrote it?" Kate asked.

"Mozart," said Loretta.

Mozart? The great composer had been dead for two hundred years. And Austria was a very long way from Texas.

But through Loretta's grandmother, Kate supposed it was possible a tiny, rare piece of him had landed here. If so, it would be incredibly valuable. More than that, it was exciting to think of touching a sheet of music actually penned by that genius.

He had written the very opera for which Loretta had just auditioned. How ironic to discover there was a special connection between the two of them, Kate thought.

The younger woman poked behind the hanging clothes. Her breath caught audibly.

"It's there?" Kate asked.

"I think so." With infinite care, Loretta lifted out several oversize, yellowing sheets lined with hand-drawn staffs. "'*La Speranza di Amore*,'" she whispered. "'The Hope of Love.'"

"What is it?" Kate counted two, no, three sheets of paper. "Part of an opera?"

"It's a song."

"I've never heard of it."

"No one's ever heard of it," Loretta breathed. "Not these days, anyway."

"An unknown song by Mozart? It must be worth—"

"Millions," said a nasal male voice from the outer room.

Alarm jolted through Kate and for the moment she couldn't react. Loretta shook so hard she nearly dropped the manuscript.

The man who walked in had a sharp nose, a receding hairline and a thickening waist. Feral intelligence glittered in his eyes.

"Billy!" Loretta gaped at him. "Uh, hello. We were just—I forgot to take—"

"What you came here to search for." The man sneered. "I figured you must be after something, Loretta. I was waiting for you to lead me to it."

He must have entered the tornado shelter while they were getting the trunk open. Was it simply bad luck that he'd returned early from church, or...?

In El Paso, Loretta had gone out alone once and come back with a couple of magazines. It hadn't occurred to Kate that her companion might have been careless and charged them.

That would be all it took. Once Billy Parkinson learned Loretta was in Texas, he would have been watching for her.

"You haven't introduced me to your friend." The man blocked their escape, standing with legs apart. He wore a gun in a holster.

Kate squared her shoulders. "I'm Kate Bingham, sheriff of Grazer's County, California. Loretta comes from my jurisdiction."

"And I'm supposed to believe you're here on business?" taunted the man. "You got a warrant, sheriff?"

He'd caught them dead to rights. Still, Loretta was only trying to take something she believed was part of her inheritance.

"I think we can get this straightened out to your satisfaction, Mr. Parkinson," Kate said. "If we've caused any damage, I'll be happy to pay for it."

"First, I'll take that." He held out his hand for the music.

Loretta clutched it to her chest. "Absolutely not! This meant something special to my grandmother. She sang it once in a concert in Milan."

"I'm not big on sentiment." Billy stepped toward her. "If you won't give me what's mine, I might have to burn it. Along with the rest of the stuff your grandmother left. And any intruders that just unfortunately happen to be in here when the place catches fire."

It struck Kate that this man had no intention of letting them get away, even if Loretta did give him the music. He'd thought out his plan too clearly.

"What about your friends?" she asked, trying to stall to give herself time to figure out what to do next. "Tiny Wheeler's gang. Are they going to be a party to murder?"

In view of the fact that these very men had tried to shoot her and Mitch several times, she didn't suppose they would quibble about killing her and Loretta. But she wanted to know if she was dealing with one man or four. If she could delay Billy until his employees came home...

"They got held up in Santa Fe with a little medical problem, but I'm expecting them any minute." Billy removed the pistol from its holster. "Don't worry, girls. I can handle the two of you myself."

Kate would have leaped at him, if she could be sure Loretta would seize the chance to escape. At least one of them might survive that way. If a fire broke out in this enclosed space, neither of them had a chance.

But the other woman wasn't thinking about out how to save her life. She was clutching the manuscript and staring at the cowboy in disgust.

"You set me up!" she said. "All that stuff about how much you liked me? You're nothing but a liar!"

"What about you?" He gave a disdainful laugh. "A broken heart that sent you scurrying back to home-sweet-home on the range?"

"Okay, you're even," Kate said. "Let's go outside and she'll give you the manuscript."

"I won't!"

"You will," Kate said. "Outside."

"Unfortunately, there's one other little matter,"

Billy said. "Our nosy friend here had a bad habit of sneaking around. That means there's no telling what she might have overheard."

"Such as you planning to lure Mitch onto your ranch and shoot him, then pretend you'd interrupted a break-in?" Kate hoped Loretta was getting the point. *We have to get outside. This man is a killer.*

"I didn't hear them planning anything." The younger woman sounded dazed.

"Even if you didn't, you might say you did to save that cousin of yours," snarled Billy.

"You think I'd lie to a jury?" A pinch of color returned to Loretta's cheeks. "You think I'm dishonest because you are, don't you? Mitch was right. You *did* steal the ranch. I don't know how, but you must have. You don't know how to do anything decent."

From outside, Kate heard a car door slam. Then another. The Tiny Wheeler gang must have arrived. She had to act now.

"Get out!" She shoved Loretta forward and to one side, hoping she would dodge around Billy.

The younger woman stumbled. Billy snatched the music from her hand, shoved it into his belt and raised the pistol.

Covering them both, he edged back through the outer room. "I'm sure my boys would like to say goodbye to you ladies, but they have an unfortunate tendency to trip over their own feet." With one hand, he untwisted the lid from a metal container. Gasoline fumes filled the room.

"You wouldn't..." Loretta caught her balance by stepping in front of Kate. "That's too horrible!"

"We've got to rush him!" But the younger woman was blocking her.

With a flick of the wrist, Billy tossed the container's contents onto the boxes. Then he reached into his pocket and drew out a lighter.

That was when a dark shape came flying through the door behind him. With a curse, Billy fell to his knees.

Kate couldn't see their rescuer clearly, but her heart knew him at once. It was Mitch.

Chapter Fourteen

Thrilled as she was to see Mitch, Kate knew he could die in here. They all could. It wouldn't take much of a spark to set the place ablaze.

While he struggled with Billy, her first job was to get Loretta to safety. Grabbing the young woman's arm, Kate hauled her forward.

The two men plunged by, narrowly missing the women. Loretta reached out and grabbed something from Billy's belt.

It was the song for which she'd risked her life. All their lives.

And then they were outside at the foot of the steps, blinking at the intensity of the midday sun. Kate sucked in great breaths of the sweet air.

"Go on!" she said. "I've got to help Mitch."

But someone was descending toward them. A big, beefy man wearing a furious scowl.

"Chief Novo!" Loretta wavered at the bottom of the steps. "What are you doing here?"

Kate's heart sank. The man was Billy's friend and, judging by the ambush in Oak Creek Canyon, his accomplice.

To her surprise, he moved aside and let Loretta pass. "You must be Kate," he said. "Get on up there."

"But Mitch—"

The chief frowned as he caught a whiff from inside the shelter. "Is that gasoline?"

From the top of the stairs, Loretta called, "I can see the van coming up the drive! It's Tiny Wheeler!"

Chief Novo muttered an oath. "I've got to head them off. Fetch the hose, you two! That place could go up like a tinderbox!"

He took off at top speed. Kate ran to get the hose, which lay tangled in a heap at the back of the house. After tucking the sheet music onto the rear porch, Loretta hurried to help her.

It took an agonizing length of time to unknot the mess. Kate kept expecting to hear the blast of gunshots or, worse, smell the choking harshness of fire.

Finally she yanked out the last kink and Loretta tossed her the nozzle. "Go ahead! I'll turn it on."

"Full force!" Grasping the hose under her arm, Kate pounded toward the shelter.

As she reached the entrance, she heard masculine grunts and the thud of bodies. Thank goodness, they were both still alive.

"Here goes!" cried Loretta.

The hose inflated with the weight of the water. Kate reached to twist the nozzle into the On position.

Her hand wrenched at the metal, in vain. The thing was jammed.

She planted herself in the stairwell to get a better grip. A scuffling noise from inside startled her, and then Mitch shouted "Move!" barely in time for Kate to jump out of the way.

Through the entrance lunged the two men. Billy fell

backward, hit the steps with a painful crack and lay still.

Mitch stood over him, breathing hard. His chin bled from a scrape, his upper lip was swollen and one cheek had begun turning a spectacular shade of purple. A yoked blue shirt clung to his broad shoulders and heaving chest, and raw fury blazed from eyes the color of molten gold.

Kate had never seen, never dreamed of such pure masculine power. None of Agatha Flintstone's knights in shining armor could ever have looked so devastating.

To her amazement, in spite of what she'd just been through, she yearned to drag the man into the barn, pull off those sweat-soaked clothes and thank him every way she could for saving her life.

Instead, she lifted the hose and said, ''Want a shower?''

''Not in my face, thank you, Fireman Kate.'' With a crooked grin, he hoisted Billy's inert body up the steps and onto the weedy ground.

''I'd better dilute that gasoline before the whole place goes up.'' She gritted her teeth and, using her shirttail to get better traction, grasped the nozzle.

''Don't go inside!''

''I'm not stupid.'' She yanked, hard, and finally twisted the nozzle. Water spewed in through the door.

Some of the outer room's contents might suffer damage, but it couldn't be helped. At least, Kate thought, most of Grandma Luisa's treasures could be saved.

Mitch prodded Billy with his boot to make sure the man wasn't regaining consciousness, then came to take the hose. "Where's Novo? He was right behind me."

As she reached the top of the stairwell, Kate spotted Loretta standing to one side, peering past the house and down toward the front drive. The younger woman responded with a thumbs-up signal.

"Apparently he's just captured the Tiny Wheeler gang." As Kate spoke, she heard a tremor in her voice. Then she realized her knees were shaking, too. "I feel funny."

"You're not going to faint, are you?" Mitch turned toward her, momentarily forgetting to watch the hose. Until, that is, water crashed against the front of the shelter. It bounced off and enveloped them in a fine, cold spray.

Kate started to laugh, and found that she wanted to cry, too, but she wasn't sure why. It was a relief when Mitch turned off the nozzle, and then she heard eager shouts coming from the far side of the hill.

The ranch hands had returned from church in time to give Mitch a warm welcome, and assist Chief Novo in bringing everything under control.

IT WAS SEVERAL hours before the tumult died down.

A fire crew arrived, summoned by the chief, and hauled half the contents of the tornado shelter into the yard. The local doctor took charge of Billy, who had suffered a concussion but would recover to face charges.

There would be two counts of attempted murder stemming from that day's events. And, after all three of his accomplices broke down under questioning, he faced further charges in the death of Jules Kominsky.

The gang members were wanted in Arizona in connection with the pileup in Oak Creek Canyon, and of course in Grazer's Corners. It would be up to the respective district attorneys to work out who got them first.

The reign of Billy Parkinson and the Tiny Wheeler gang at the High C Ranch had come to an inglorious end.

Although the title to the land remained unclear, no one objected when Mitch, Kate and Loretta stayed at the house after the police and firefighters left. It was a good thing, because, even after her shivering wore off, Kate didn't want to go anywhere or do anything except stay close to Mitch.

The three of them retreated to the living room. Loretta, suffering from a delayed reaction, huddled in a love seat with a comforter wrapped around her.

Kate nestled on the couch and gazed through the bay window at the ranch spread out below. Green land patched with shrubs and etched with fences stretched into the dusty distance. Cattle and horses clustered placidly near a stream that sparkled in the June sunshine.

No wonder Mitch's grandfather had chosen this site to build his home. Its pastoral view brought peace, slowly but surely, seeping into Kate's turbulent soul.

Towering above her as he paced the floor, Mitch seemed different from the man she had come to know these past weeks. No longer a fugitive, watchful and restrained, but lord of the manor, his mind filled with responsibilities.

Kate could feel his attention shift across the landscape from a broken fence to a potholed trail. All the way up to a sagging trellis that stood by the front porch, and a climbing rose grown scraggly from neglect.

A lot of work needed to be done as soon as he regained his deed, and he must be eager to get started. This was a magnificent ranch.

Part of Kate's heart belonged here with him. And part of it was firmly lodged back in Grazer's Corners, the town that had always been home, and especially at the school that still needed her.

She decided not to think about it today. She just wanted to sit here and delight in the fact that all three of them were safe. And that Mitch, whatever the future might bring, was no longer a wanted man.

Not wanted except by her, she admitted with a sigh. And she wanted him with every fiber in her body. Wanted to kiss the bruises from his face and strip away those dusty clothes and heal them both in the most elemental way.

But this wasn't the moment. Especially not with Loretta so uncharacteristically pale. Once the fact had sunk in that they'd nearly died, she had withdrawn into herself, not even glancing at the sheet music she'd set on a table beside her.

"You haven't told us how you came to bring the cavalry to our rescue," Kate said, almost as interested in piquing Loretta's curiosity as in satisfying her own.

A moment passed. Then Mitch turned away from the window, blinking as if newly awakened. "I'm sorry. I've been noticing how badly Billy let the place run down."

"Maybe we can use the building supplies he left." Loretta perked up. "Mario's good at carpentry. It's thanks to him the place isn't in even worse shape."

Gingerly, Mitch lowered himself onto the split upholstery of an easy chair. "I hope you'll stick around for a while and make suggestions. It's going to take me a while to get my mind focused on running a ranch again."

"I'd love to." Loretta let the comforter slide from her shoulders. "So, how *did* you get Chief Novo on your side?"

"Well," Mitch said, "it all started when I walked into the church and the pastor looked up and said, 'Ah, the prodigal son has come home.'"

OVER A HUNDRED FACES had turned toward him. But where Mitch had feared to see disgust or anger, he saw mostly sympathy and support.

The townspeople believed in him. That fact buoyed him on as he announced, "I've come to turn myself in. But first I want everyone to know that if I die in custody, don't believe any stories about me trying to escape or attacking the police chief. You see, he's already tried once to have me killed."

Chief Novo hadn't denied it, or blustered. He had stood to face Mitch and said, "What the hell are you talking about?"

Mitch told him, and the assembled worshipers-turned-witnesses, about his search for Sarah Rosen in Oak Creek Canyon, and how he'd been ambushed. As he spoke, the chief's face darkened with fury.

"I never set you up," he said. "It was Billy. I told him where you were going, but I never... Where is he? Anybody seen him today?"

No one had. Then a rancher mentioned spotting Loretta's car heading for the High C.

"She was looking for something valuable," Mitch said. "I guess she's trying to sneak back onto the premises. Billy might have figured it out and set her up."

And Kate, he had thought with a rush of panic. *Kate would have stayed with her, if she knew Loretta was coming back.*

"What are you waiting for?" the chief had demanded. "Let's hightail it over there!"

And so they had.

"Thank goodness you came when you did," Kate said.

The filtered sunlight gave her face a warm glow, or perhaps it came from within. Mitch had to fight the impulse to take that defiant chin in his hand, and kiss her until they both forgot how tired and dirty they were.

But he couldn't. He had too many things to sort out, deep inside.

Like the fact that when he'd driven onto the ranch ahead of Chief Novo, he had felt nothing at all for this place that had haunted and obsessed him for the past ten years. The only thought in his mind had been that he couldn't bear to lose Kate.

He'd wrenched open his door as soon as the truck stopped, and hit the ground at a run. A roaring abyss had opened in his gut at the realization that if he failed Kate, nothing would ever have meaning for him again.

And now? Mitch still cared about this place, his family home. He knew its scents and textures in his soul, and he felt an obligation to claim it and restore it.

What he no longer knew was himself. Who he was. What he wanted from life. And until he did, he had no right to make demands on Kate.

"I don't believe it!" The cry from Loretta jerked

him from his reflections. His cousin had picked up the top page of the yellowing manuscript and was squinting at it.

"It's damaged?" Kate asked. "Surely it can be restored."

Loretta shook her head. "No, it isn't that. It's...it's not by Mozart."

Mitch hadn't paid much attention to the explanation Kate had given him earlier, about his cousin's quest. Now he recalled something about Grandma Luisa bringing the song from Italy more than fifty years ago.

"Well, that's hardly surprising," he said. "How would she have come by such an old, rare piece of music? Not to mention the fact that Mozart was Austrian, not Italian."

"But she told me..." Loretta chewed on her lip. "I guess she was delirious. Or I misunderstood."

"Who did write it?" Kate asked. "It's obviously an original piece of music."

The younger woman touched the edge of the paper lightly, as if trying to reassure it, or herself, that all was not lost. "It's by a composer named Pietro Mascagni. He was a conductor that she worked with at La Scala—I remember her telling me. He died several years later."

"He also wrote operas. His best known is *Cavalleria Rusticana,* or *Rustic Chivalry,*" Mitch recalled. "The music is beautiful. Grandma played her recording until it was all scratched."

"The composer knew your grandmother?" Kate said. "You mean he might actually have written this song for her? It might not be worth as much money as a Mozart, but as for sentimental value, I think that's even better."

Loretta dropped the sheet onto the table. "I guess I was counting on making a discovery, something that would make people notice me. And my voice."

Uncoiling from the chair, Mitch crossed and picked up the papers. They felt fragile in his hands, and he noticed several torn places.

"*La Speranza di Amore,*" the song was called. The hope of love.

The composer must have greatly admired Grandma's voice, and her spirit as well, to write it for her. Perhaps it had been composed in honor of her decision to abandon her career and risk everything for love.

As Mitch glanced over the music, a melody began to play in his mind. Startled, he realized that his grandmother must have hummed this tune or sung it at the piano when he was growing up.

It took only a glance at the spidery writing to bring the words to mind, even though they were in Italian. Without realizing it, he had come to know the piece by heart.

Oddly, this composition brought from the Old World to the new made him feel connected in a way he'd missed when he arrived at the ranch today. It had been important to his grandmother, when she began her life anew, to carry with her a precious reminder of the past.

Mitch wasn't sure why he felt so moved. He needed time to think about it.

He needed time to think about a lot of things.

BY MIDMORNING ON Monday, Mitch had a good idea of the work that lay ahead. That was, once he proved his claim to the ranch, which might present some problems.

But he still didn't know what he intended to do about Kate. Home on the range no longer sounded so appealing, but neither did he relish the prospect of spending his life cooped in an office, polishing clauses and researching nitpicks in the law.

After meeting with Mario, he returned to the ranch house. There he showered, put on a suit and tie, and went to find the ladies.

There was no sign of Kate. Loretta sat at the breakfast table nibbling on toast and reading a copy of *Farm & Ranch Living* magazine.

She took in his lawyer clothes. "Going to your office?"

"The bank, actually." He leaned against the counter. "There's a little matter of Doc Rosen's bank account that I need to clear up."

"It's obvious that Billy stole the ranch!" Loretta stormed. "Why should you have to prove anything?"

"Because what seems obvious doesn't always turn out to be true," Mitch reminded her.

His cousin ruffled a hand through her chestnut hair. "I guess I haven't said yet that I'm sorry. Well, I am. I wish I'd confided in you from the beginning."

"And I wish I'd communicated better," he said.

They smiled at each other. "I was just a kid ten years ago," Loretta said. "And in some ways, I'm beginning to realize, so were you."

It seemed so natural to see her sitting here, where their grandmother used to sit. The place must be nearly as full of memories for Loretta as for him.

But there were other memories in Mitch's heart, newer ones full of still-unresolved emotions. With a jolt, he realized his mind was viewing another kitchen, one with flowers stenciled on the walls and lace curtains at the windows.

Kate's home. Would he ever see it again?

"I've been thinking," his cousin continued. "I really love this place."

"As much as you love music?" he teased.

To his surprise, she didn't laugh off the comment. "Singing is my passion, but that's a hard life. It's competitive and it's insecure."

"Isn't that part of the fun?"

Loretta set down the magazine, her serious expression making her look older. Grown-up, even. "You worry about losing your voice, about not learning a role in time, about having some critic trash you. You jet all over the world, sometimes on short notice, if you're lucky enough to get a role at all. I think it could get hard to find your balance."

"But it's what you've always wanted." Mitch frowned. "Your voice is an amazing gift."

"I'm not quitting," his cousin assured him. "But I was fantasizing about discovering this Mozart song, giving concerts with it and getting famous just like that. Now I have to take my chances like everybody else. I'm still game to try, but I want the ranch to come home to."

There was a point that needed to be put right. "You can live here part-time or full-time, whatever you like. The ranch is half yours, and I intend to put that on the deed."

Clear eyes met his. "Thanks, Mitch. And you can count on me. I plan to be just as involved in the renovations and the day-to-day work as you are. Or Kate. You are going to marry her, aren't you?"

He couldn't give an answer, not yet. "Where is she, by the way?"

"She went into town," Loretta replied. "To get some household supplies. And I think she wanted privacy to make a phone call back home."

Mitch's fists clenched. Kate was calling Moose. He had no right to interfere, but he didn't give a damn.

He loved the woman. He had to tell her, had to win her, had to prevent her from marrying that idiot.

Grabbing his hat, he clapped it onto his head. "I'll see you later."

"Good luck," Loretta said.

He wasn't sure whether she meant at the bank, or with Kate. Both, he thought. He needed luck with both.

Chapter Fifteen

Kate couldn't believe she was standing in a shop window making the most important phone call of her life.

When she'd decided to drive into town to pick up some personal items, it had seemed like a good idea to find a pay phone. That way, she wouldn't feel inhibited by the possibility that Mitch might overhear.

Not that she planned to say anything she didn't want him to know. But breaking off with Moose was her own decision, free and clear of anything that might happen between her and Mitch. She didn't want him to feel responsible.

What she hadn't counted on was that small towns didn't exactly sport pay phones on every corner. Gulch City appeared to have only one, at the gas station, and it had been monopolized for the past half hour by a trucker with a bad case of honey-I-miss-you-itis.

In frustration, she'd inquired at the pharmacy. They didn't have a pay phone, but the sympathetic owner had offered to lend her a regular one with a long extension cord, if she bought a calling card to pay the toll charges.

And so here Kate stood, flanked on one side by the high counter and, on the other, by a plate glass window displaying this week's special on trusses. She wasn't exactly in full view of the town, but this hardly qualified as privacy, either.

However, the owner was listening to country music on a headset and there was no one else in the store. She supposed it was less public than standing in front of the gas station, and not nearly as smelly.

It was 10:15 a.m. Texas time, but only 8:15 back in California. Kate tried Moose at home.

Listening to the first ring, she got a twitchy feeling in her stomach. What exactly was she going to say? How would he take it?

On the second ring, someone picked up. "Hello?" said a woman.

For a moment, Kate couldn't catch her bearings. Then she said, "I must have misdialed."

"What number were you calling?" To Kate's hypersensitive ears, the woman sounded uncomfortable. And a little familiar, but she couldn't place the voice.

Kate recited Moose's number.

"Uh…" The woman coughed. "Were you trying to reach Moose?"

"This *is* Moose Harmon's house?" As if there were likely to be someone else named Moose with a similar phone number!

But Kate couldn't imagine who the woman was. Moose had hired a cleaning service, not a housekeeper, and he didn't have a sister.

"Kate?" said the woman. "Ohmigosh. Moose! Moose! It's Kate!"

A loud *Bang!* indicated the phone had been dropped onto a hard surface. Lovely, Kate thought. How strange, Kate thought. And then: *Either I'm hallucinating or the world has turned upside down.*

The phone rasped as it was picked up. "Uh, Kate?" Moose sounded hoarse.

"Did I wake you?"

"No, no, I was in the shower. Uh...where are you?"

"Texas." Kate tried to shut out the image that sprang to mind, of Moose's oversize frame wrapped in a bath towel, dripping water onto the floor. "Who was that woman?"

He cleared his throat. "I'll ask the questions around here, thank you."

Now he sounded more like himself. That didn't mean she had to let him push her around, however. "I've wrapped up the case," Kate said. "Mitch Connery has been cleared of murder charges."

"No kidding? You really solved a case?"

"I did." Not all by herself, but this was no time for modesty.

"Boy, we sure could have used you around here, with all those other kidnappings," he said.

"What do you mean?" Kidnappings? In Grazer's Corners?

"You should have been here, Kate!" he enthused. "I've never seen anything like it! Three weekends in a row, three different weddings shot to...well, it's all working itself out, I guess. Anyhow, you'd think people would have enough to gossip about without..." He stopped as if he'd been on the verge of revealing too much. "Some people are small-minded, that's all I can say."

Kate wondered if this conversation was being bounced off a satellite and, en route, overheard by aliens. If so, they probably understood it about as well as she did.

Through the window, she noticed that Mitch's camper-laden pickup was parked in front of the bank. A pang of nostalgia shot through her as memories crowded back. A rainy night in the middle of nowhere...a cookout in Santa Fe...

"Kate?" Moose prompted. "You still there?"

"Some people are small-minded about what?" she asked. "You mean about that woman you're sleeping with?"

He gasped. "Kate!"

"Why else would she be there at eight-fifteen in the morning, while you were taking a shower?"

A relieved sigh came across the phone. "I should have known you'd figure it out. Listen, I didn't plan this, believe me. But you *did* leave me at the altar. In fact, it was downright embarrassing, you running off with that man! You can hardly blame me for accepting a little comfort from someone else!"

"Is it Betsy?" she said.

"Uh, yes."

"I hope you'll both be very happy."

"You're not mad?" Moose asked.

"Not at all." In fact, if Betsy were standing here, Kate would have thrown her arms around the woman and thanked her.

"Really? That's great. Oh, one more thing, Kate."

"What's that?"

"I'm resigning as mayor." A note of hurt crept into his voice. "Like I said, people can be so petty!"

"About Betsy?"

"Sure. And not having a professional band to play in the park. And you disappearing. Everything. They're always whining. I'm tired of shouldering everyone else's burdens." He was picking up steam.

"Including yours! It's time you got back here and hired a professional deputy, like we agreed!"

She hadn't exactly agreed; she'd been bulldozed. But that no longer seemed important. "I'll take care of it. Give Betsy my best, Moose."

"I'm right here!" chirped a female voice on the extension. "Thanks, Kate! You're a great sport!"

"Get off the phone, Betsy!" roared Moose.

"Bye," said Kate, and hung up before she found herself in the middle of somebody else's argument.

She felt an odd mixture of liberation and sadness. After all these years, Moose had dumped her with scarcely a second thought.

On the other hand, she'd dumped him, too. But in a way, Kate envied him. He and Betsy worked together. They shared a hometown, although perhaps not the same friends. It would be relatively easy enough to work things out.

Not like her and Mitch.

But we will, she thought with a spurt of determination. *If he really wants to.*

Then she glanced out the window again and saw something utterly strange. And wonderful.

Mitch stood in the middle of Main Street with a guitar looped over his shoulder, like a troubadour. He was staring through the glass at her.

When their eyes met, he strummed a couple of chords and began to sing. The song reached her muffled but rich with his baritone, and his longing.

For a heartbeat, Kate couldn't move. Then, stiffly, as if she'd been given the body of a stranger, she walked to the pharmacy's open door.

Behind her, she heard the owner say, "Ain't that Mitch Connery? Why's he singin' in Eye-talian?"

She stepped onto the sidewalk. Now she could hear him clearly. So could the whole town.

A woman with a baby carriage stood transfixed. Two dirty-faced little boys stopped bouncing a ball to listen. Outside the video rental store, an elderly woman holding a copy of *Sense and Sensibility* paused with bliss radiating from her still-youthful eyes.

Mitch's tall, confident body dominated the street, the town, the world. His face shone with hope and tenderness and a hint of wistful uncertainty as his warm voice filled the empty spaces of Kate's soul.

It was the most beautiful song she had ever heard, because she knew it was for her. She only understood one word, *amore,* but that was enough.

The melody ended, much too soon. From the sidewalk and the shops came a scattering of applause. Mitch didn't seem to notice.

Never taking his gaze from hers, he went down on one knee, right in the middle of the street. It was a good thing they didn't have much traffic in Gulch City.

"Kate Bingham," he said, "will you marry me?"

Her breath caught in her throat, and for a moment she couldn't speak.

"You have to say yes," said the lady with the baby. "Or you'll ruin my day."

"Of course she'll say yes." The elderly woman hugged the tape. "If she doesn't, she'll regret it all her life."

Kate nodded. "Yes," she whispered.

"Louder," said Mitch.

"Louder?"

"I'm not sure I heard you."

"Yes!" she cried, and ran into the street. He barely

stood up in time to catch her, and then he had to turn sideways or risk hitting her with his guitar.

"Yes!" she shouted again.

He folded her against him. A panel delivery truck turned a corner, and Mitch steered them both to the sidewalk, half-carrying her. The townspeople discreetly went about their business, smiling and humming.

"I broke up with Moose," she said, holding on with all her might. She couldn't wait to get this man alone. Her husband-to-be. The one she'd always been meant to marry. "Mitch, we'll work something out, about where to live. We need to talk things over, think about it, maybe experiment a little."

"That won't be necessary," he said. "I still love the ranch but it isn't my home. My home is where you are."

It was exactly what she wanted to hear. But Kate couldn't let Mitch sacrifice everything he'd worked for, these past ten years.

"How can you do that?" she asked. "It means so much to you, and Loretta."

He chuckled. "I think we swapped goals. She got the ranch and I got the song. Kate, I haven't been a cowboy for a decade. I was so fixated on regaining the ranch, I never stopped to think about whether I could be happy there after all this time. Now that I've got it back..."

"You have?" she asked.

Mitch held out the bankbook, the one they'd gotten from Sarah Rosen. Curious, she flipped it open.

The entries had been updated. Beginning with the previous balance of fifteen years ago, someone had made monthly deposits of several hundred dollars for the next four years.

They ended eleven years ago. After that, deposits of one dollar showed up yearly.

"Your dad paid off the loan into the doctor's account?" Kate said. "What about these one dollar deposits?"

"The banker's young. He took over for his father, and he never connected Doc Rosen's unclaimed account with Billy Parkinson seizing the ranch," Mitch explained. "But he didn't want the account to go dormant, so when he couldn't reach Sarah Rosen, he started putting in a dollar of his own money every year to keep it alive."

"Here's your proof!" Kate said. "Your Dad didn't default."

Mitch nodded. "Not only that, but there's a hefty balance. I'm sure Sarah can use it. That banker felt great when I told him how much this would mean to her."

They started toward the pickup truck. "You're going to give the ranch to Loretta?" Kate asked.

"Half of it, anyway." He held the door for her. "I'd like for you and me to spend summers here, if I can take the time off from my law clients."

"Law clients?"

He put the guitar in back and came around to the driver's seat. "I figure Grazer's Corners could probably use another attorney."

"It could use a sheriff even more," she said.

Sunlight raised golden gleams in his eyes. "I thought you were the sheriff."

"I'd like to hire you as my deputy." The idea sprang into her brain full-blown. "The town can pay for your training and, once you're up to speed, I'll stand down in your favor. I'm sure you'll get elected.''

"The husband of the school principal and all that?" he murmured as he started the engine.

"The best darn sheriff the town's ever had, and all *that*," she corrected.

He backed out and straightened the truck. She wondered if he was going to refuse.

It was up to him, Kate told herself as they rumbled out of town. As long as she had Mitch's gentle understanding to rely on, and his arms around her at night, and his mouth tracing fire along her breasts, and his body hard and tender as he drove every rational thought from her brain...

Well, as long as she had those things, she didn't need to run his life. Just because the man was perfect for the job, that didn't mean he had to take it.

They had nearly reached the ranch before he spoke again.

"I guess being wrongly accused of murder does give a man a certain insight," Mitch said slowly. "You know, I think I'd enjoy being on the right side of the law for a change. I'm kind of looking forward to getting started."

It was too bad he'd probably be too late to solve the recent rash of kidnappings. But Kate had a feeling there'd be plenty of other matters to investigate.

Moose had once said that nothing ever happened in Grazer's Corners. Well, everyone was entitled to be wrong once in a while.

As they parked at the house, Kate could see Loretta and Mario far down the slope, heading out onto the range in a four-wheel-drive vehicle. Beside her, she heard Mitch singing beneath his breath.

It was the song with which he'd serenaded her: *"La Speranza di Amore."* The hope of love.

Except now they had more than just hope.

He came around to lift her down, and they walked to the house, both humming the tune. And laughing. And hurrying to get inside, where they had important things to talk about, and even more important things to do that didn't require talking at all.

THE BRIDES

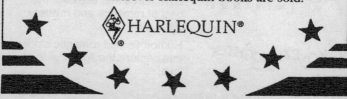

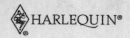

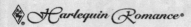

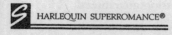

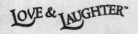

MEN at WORK

All work and no play?
Not these men!

July 1998

MACKENZIE'S LADY by Dallas Schulze

Undercover agent Mackenzie Donahue's
lazy smile and deep blue eyes were his best
weapons. But after rescuing—and kissing!—
damsel in distress Holly Reynolds, how could
he betray her by spying on her brother?

August 1998

MISS LIZ'S PASSION by Sherryl Woods

Todd Lewis could put up a building with ease,
but quailed at the sight of a classroom! Still,
Liz Gentry, his son's teacher, was no battle-ax,
and soon Todd started planning some
extracurricular activities of his own....

September 1998

A CLASSIC ENCOUNTER
by Emilie Richards

Doctor Chris Matthews was intelligent, sexy
and *very* good with his hands—which made
him all the more dangerous to single mom
Lizette St. Hilaire. So how long could she
resist Chris's special brand of TLC?

Available at your favorite retail outlet!

MEN AT WORK™

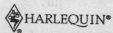 HARLEQUIN®    Silhouette®

Look us up on-line at: http://www.romance.net

PMAW2

DEBBIE MACOMBER

invites you to the

HEART OF TEXAS

Join Debbie Macomber as she brings you the lives
and loves of the folks in the ranching community
of Promise, Texas.

If you loved Midnight Sons—don't miss
Heart of Texas! A brand-new six-book series
from Debbie Macomber.

Available in February 1998
at your favorite retail store.

Heart of Texas by Debbie Macomber

Lonesome Cowboy	February '98
Texas Two-Step	March '98
Caroline's Child	April '98
Dr. Texas	May '98
Nell's Cowboy	June '98
Lone Star Baby	July '98

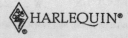
HARLEQUIN®

Heat up your summer this July with

Summer Lovers

This July, bestselling authors Barbara Delinsky,
Elizabeth Lowell and Anne Stuart present three
couples with pasts that threaten their future happiness.
Can they play with fire without being burned?

FIRST, BEST AND ONLY
by Barbara Delinsky

GRANITE MAN
by Elizabeth Lowell

CHAIN OF LOVE
by Anne Stuart

Available wherever Harlequin and Silhouette books
are sold.

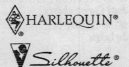

HARLEQUIN®

Silhouette®

COMING NEXT MONTH

#737 DADDY BY DEFAULT by Muriel Jensen
Who's the Daddy?
When Darrick McKeon—the man she never got over—returns with twin babies, demanding if she is the mystery woman who named him as the babies' father and then disappeared, Skye Fennery knows all that stands between her and happiness is a little white lie. So she decides to *make* them a family—if only temporarily.

#738 DREAM BABY by Emily Dalton
Maggie Stern wants nothing to do with her new neighbor, the handsome yet forbidding pediatrician Jared Austin. But then a fan leaves a baby on the doorstep for the infertile character Maggie plays on TV and suddenly she has nowhere else to turn....

#739 A BACHELOR FOR THE BRIDE by Mindy Neff
The Brides of Grazer's Corners
To save her family from disaster Jordan Grazer had to go through with her wedding. But then Tanner Caldwell roared into town and whisked her away for sensuous kisses under the stars. Nothing could make Jordan go back home...except her own promise to say "I do."

#740 TUESDAY'S KNIGHT by Julie Kistler
Kally Malone had always had her life firmly in control. Not anymore! Tim's obsidian eyes and fiery kisses made her all jittery.... And her daughter, Tuesday—seven going on thirty—had a mission: to make Tim part of their family...as the daddy.

AVAILABLE THIS MONTH:

Look us up on-line at: http://www.romance.net